GETTING A LIFE

by

Helen Cammuso,
A.J. Kelly,
Dee Greenberg

First published by AuthorHouse 12/07/04

ISBN: 1-4184-1886-2 (e-book)
ISBN: 1-4184-1887-0 (Paperback)

Printed in the United States of America
Bloomington, IN

Library of Congress Control Number: 2004092232

This book is printed on acid free paper.

To the memory of

David Romaine Bohme

TABLE OF CONTENTS

ACKNOWLEDGEMENTS

We are each grateful for the support our husbands gave us during this project. As always, they believed in us, and in our writing.

We thank Shirley O'Rourke for her interest in the book. Her comments and suggestions were helpful.

We must also mention The Little Corner Snack Shop, where we spent many hours expanding on our creations.

Most of all, we thank one another for the encouragement, and sharing experience. Without that, this book wouldn't have been possible.

HELEN CAMMUSO - About The Author

HELEN began writing when she was a grandmother. She has worked as a copy-writer and had stories published in *Mature Lifestyles*, a paper in Madison, Wisconsin. Helen lives in Chicago with her husband Michael, who is an artist.

CROSSROADS

Lorenzo Aprile barely listened to the group's faltering discussion about impotency. Their voices eddied past him like soft static as he wrestled with his own thoughts. Early in the session he knew that what they said was bullshit. He hadn't leveled with the support group since he came back to the Blind Center for a refresher course in mobility training. How could he possibly tell them he wanted to divorce Angie after forty-three years of marriage?

"Lorenzo, what do you think?" Dr. Schroeder caught him completely off guard.

"About what, Doctor, I missed that."

"Marty just said that he and Ruth are sixty-five now and sex isn't as important to them as it once was."

Lorenzo shifted his weight uneasily on his metal chair, which was as uncomfortable as the subject matter.

"Marty is lucky to have someone like Ruth who shares so much more than sex with him."

Lorenzo and Marty Swartz had served in the same Division in the Korean War and both had faithfully attended five-year reunions of the Third Armored Division since then. He knew Marty and Ruth well. They were both teachers and had everything in common. They had the best marriage of anyone he knew.

Ruth was nothing like Angie. Nothing. He had seen Ruth before diabetes robbed both him and Marty of their sight. Ruth was a plain woman, definitely not a beauty like Angie. At sixty-two, Angie was as lovely as the day they were married. Lorenzo had fallen in love with her Botticelli face, her shapely figure and energetic good spirits. As his disease progressed and his diminishing sight had all but obscured that face and figure, Lorenzo found his sexual drive waning and with it all attachment to Angie and the life they shared. Besides their family, sex was all he and Angie had in common.

"I tried to kill myself last Christmas." John Connelly, the group leader, threw out that laconic sentence, its seven words exploding like grenades, one after the other.

Lorenzo's white cane clattered onto the tile floor, its impact resounding like still another bomb. He barely heard Dr. Schroeder murmur:

"What stopped you?"

"Nothing stopped me! I didn't take enough fucking pills! I slept a day and a half, woke up alive and Christmas was over."

"Have you thought about it since?"

Stupid God damned shrink, Lorenzo thought as he fumbled for his cane. Just about everyday since that last bit of light faded, *I've* thought about it!

Until a year ago, in strong light, Lorenzo could make out misty shapes before his betraying eyes. Some days, Angie's beautiful face shimmered vaguely before him like a mirage on an arid desert, the details

4

always cruelly blurred, just an amorphous speck of vision, but something he desperately needed to stir the memories of life fully lived. At home in Detroit, surrounded by friends and family, Lorenzo felt completely alone.

"John, you'd say anything to change the subject. What's the matter, can't you get it up anymore?" Fat, jolly Bobby Jenkins broke the tension. Uneasy laughter spread around the circle like trickling water extinguishing a flame.

Lorenzo touched the button on his talking watch and heard its small metallic voice tell him that the session had ended.

Over the sound of rattling metal chairs, tapping canes and shuffling feet, Lorenzo heard Dr. Schroeder ask John Connelly to stay behind. Lorenzo got out of the room as fast as he could. He didn't want to think about what John Connelly had said, not now. He wanted to think about going to the weekly dance tonight, and seeing Martha Higgins.

On the way to his room he made a wrong turn on Two South. Cursing under his breath, he righted his direction and heard Bobby Jenkins call out.

"Wait up, Lor." Bobby puffed up beside him. "What's the hurry?"

"I'm going to the dance tonight and I promised Angie I'd call. You know how long that takes." He slowed his pace and Bobby caught his breath. "It's my grandson's birthday and the whole family will be with Angie tonight. Everyone will talk to me."

Indeed Angie would lead him through every detail of her day, from the selection of the food for dinner to the preparation and the baking of the birthday cake.

How he had hoped when his sight began to fail that Angie would start to share some of his interests! Maybe go to the opera once in a while or join the book club at the library, but she never had. She always threw up her hands and teased him about his high brow tastes.

Somewhere along the line his high brow tastes had become his passion, and his dream of becoming a teacher when he retired from his job at the Ford Plant became his secret ambition. That dream had died, until last year when he came to Hines Veterans Hospital and met Martha Higgins.

Bobby's room was directly across from Lorenzo's. Both men knew this part of the hospital like the backs of their hands and they stopped at exactly the same spot.

"You're going to skip the workout room tonight then?" Bobby asked and reached out and patted Lorenzo's love handles. "I think I will, too."

"Go, Bobby. Ride the bikes at least. You've got to get your weight down or you'll--"

"Or I'll what, Lor? Die?" Bobby cut in, and then laughed. The sound crackled like the lash of a worn out bull whip.

"We're lucky we have our families, eh, Lor?"

6

"Bobby, go to the gym and get John Connelly to go with you. Don't let him be alone tonight."

"Okay, Lor." Bobby sighed deeply. "But we're still going to smuggle pizza in after the dance."

Lorenzo heard Bobby's brittle laugh echoing through the empty hallway even after he closed his door.

Lorenzo made his call to Detroit. It was exactly as he had described to Bobby Jenkins and it left him as lonely and disconnected from his family as ever.

He undressed quickly and went into the shower. He lathered himself and let the beating warm water soothe and calm him. He deliberately thought of Martha and that first dance the summer before. His black mood gradually lifted and a big smile spread across his face as his thoughts drifted back.

Well meaning elderly volunteers gave their time as partners for the veterans while a disc jockey played old tapes on an outdated sound system. Martha was one of those elderly volunteers. She had asked him to dance, and when he slipped his arm around her waist, he remembered exactly what he had thought at the time, How far the mighty have fallen when Lorenzo Aprile spends Friday night dancing with a hefty stranger in a stuffy hospital recreation room!

But Martha had followed him with grace and expertise and they had danced every dance from a mellow waltz to a spirited jitterbug.

He liked Martha from the start. Her voice was soft and soothing and she smelled faintly of lilacs, Lorenzo's favorite flower. He was with her often after that. She was a retired nurse and a widow who filled the void in her life with volunteer work. She drove the patients to many of the outings provided by the Blind Center.

During the summer they went to two Shakespeare plays, several concerts and a few poetry readings at a nearby coffeehouse. Marty Swartz went to the concerts with them but most of the time they had been alone. The best times were those evenings after the readings when they sipped espresso and shyly read their own poems to each other.

Though not a word of love had passed between them, Lorenzo knew that he loved Martha Higgins and that she loved him.

Still smiling, Lorenzo stepped out of the shower and turned on the radio. He danced around the room to some soft rock as he dressed. No matter how much he tried to avoid the inevitable, he couldn't put off the decision about a divorce much longer. Angie would get along without him very well. She had a life of her own that barely included him, and she could continue to have that life without him. The scandal of divorce and whether he had the guts to face it were the reasons he hesitated to end his marriage.

When he finished dressing, he ran a comb through his still curly hair, put on his watch and headed for the dining hall. He tapped his way to Two South and hesitated a moment

8

to get his bearings before he decided which way to go. Lorenzo made the right turn this time and he took that to be a good omen.

That night, Bobby Jenkins, not John Connelly, stepped off the walking path along Fifth Avenue in front of an oncoming diesel truck and died instantly. The next night, Lorenzo asked Martha Higgins to marry him when his divorce was final and she said yes.

A FEELING IN THE BONES

If it hadn't been a bright summer day, and the foyer hadn't been flooded with light, I would have fainted when I entered my apartment. Standing inside the front door was a tall skeleton, attached to a steel rod, standing on a small trolley.

I quickly put two and two together before my knees buckled, and realized that my daughter's boyfriend, who was studying to be a medical illustrator, must have brought his work home.

I went through the living room and out onto the balcony, looked over the railing and saw Jeannie and David sunning by the pool stories below.

He had been here a lot this summer, and I knew they were getting serious, but I hoped they weren't because they were far too young to make a lasting commitment.

Jeannie was a sophomore at the Chicago Art Institute and David was in her anatomy class. They both had talent and drive, but a long way to go.

Still, I could see her upturned summer face glowed, not just from the kiss of the sun, but also from David's kiss.

Jeannie opened her eyes and saw me. She waved, got up from her lounge chair and pulled David to his feet. Smiling and waving, they left the pool area. Something momentous was about to happen! I felt it in my bones! The skeleton must have felt it, too. When I went back into the hallway and

11

looked at its skull, it was smiling. Not a macabre smile but a sly one. Maybe this is some kind of omen, I thought, as a thousand invisible feathers tickled my stomach.

It was a strange new feeling. This would be the first time any of my three children had brought someone home they intended to marry, and by then, I knew that was what they had in mind.

I felt weaker and weaker. I knew what a romantic my daughter was, and I knew she was in love with love, and not with David.

They found me in the hallway. David's earnest brown eyes made me think of my husband's eyes when we first met.

"Well, did you see it?" Jeannie beamed as she squeezed David's hand.

They looked about twelve years old instead of nineteen. They seemed to grow younger and younger, and I felt that if I looked at them long enough, they would shrink to toddlers before my eyes. I, on the other hand, felt decidedly older.

They both seized the skeleton's hand and held it up. On its third finger, left hand, was a ring; a very small diamond ring, so small it was hard to find among the knotted bones of the skeleton's ancient appendage.

They both talked at once. They planned to marry within the year, and do what Mike and I had done years before. They would find an inexpensive apartment to live in and work their way through school.

In Jeannie's youthful scenario of the shared Bohemian life, she hadn't taken into account that Mike and I were twenty-three years old when we married, with a depression and a war, in which her father had served, behind us.

Mike and I talked to them that night and asked them to wait until they had finished school before they married. They said they would get back to us.

A week later, I came home to find the skeleton in the foyer once again; the little ring on its finger.

Jeannie came out of her bedroom, her eyes brimming with tears, and told me that the engagement was off. She was giving the ring back to David. They were not getting married, and they had even agreed to see other people.

I felt a blissful release of tension that had knotted my own body for the past week.

I knew how much it hurt Jeannie to let go of her romantic dream, and my heart ached for her.

I reached out and pulled her into my arms. I looked again at the skeleton's toothy grin. The grin grew more enigmatic as I gazed. I had the feeling that the skeleton knew that this was the beginning of a new time in Jeannie's life, and mine. A small shiver danced through me. I hugged my daughter tighter and held onto her as long as I could.

SWEETS

I was pondering the proliferation of oat bran cereal on the supermarket shelves when my neighbor, Sue, eased her cart to a smooth stop next to mine.

"Mary, I was sorry to hear about Liz and Paul's divorce. They seemed like the perfect couple to me."

She meant well, but it was the first time anyone outside the family had mentioned my daughter's divorce. My stomach did a flip flop and I thought I would throw up right there in the store as I watched her maneuver her cart down the aisle and around a tall display of Kleenex.

I abandoned the cart full of groceries and left the store sobbing and walking as fast as my legs would carry me. I was home before I remembered I had left my car in the parking lot.

Hands shaking, I let myself in the house and hung up my coat. Stumbling over the oriental rug in the hallway, I lurched into the kitchen. My kitchen, my bailiwick. I love the bright strawberry wallpaper and natural wood cabinets that Dan and I used when we remodeled it after Liz and Paul were married. That was five years ago and since then, whenever I feel blue, I come here. I brew a cup of tea, sip it from my prettiest cup and I always feel better.

I was hoping that my favorite room would work its magic today as I waited for the tea to steep and my hands to stop shaking. It

15

occurred to me that I was spending more and more time in my kitchen and less time with Dan these days. He, too, was retreating more often to his basement workshop, each of us seeking his own private comfort zone, trying to accept the unhappiness that had come into our lives.

It was six months ago on Halloween night that it happened. I was babysitting my two year old grandson, Jamie. My daughter and her husband were going to a costume party dressed as Beauty and the Beast, and Liz looked lovely when she swept into the kitchen where I was preparing a snack for Jamie. She wore a pale blue gown with a gold band around the bodice. With her dark hair and blue eyes she looked like Walt Disney's Snow White.

"Wait, Mom, don't give Jamie his milk yet, I promised him a tea party tonight." She took a small faux blue tea set from a handsome open hutch and set it on the tray of Jamie's high chair.

"Remember this, Mom?" she said as she poured milk into the little porcelain pot. "I must have been about Jamie's age when you gave me this."

She handed Jamie the pot and helped him pour the milk into three tiny cups. We watched him painstakingly put cream and sugar in our tea while we nibbled cookies from his trick or treat cache.

"I'd give anything to find a large tea set like this one for the house I'm doing now." Liz gently traced the pattern on the tea pot with her finger.

16

"Has it been hard working full time again, Liz? Being a decorator isn't an easy life."

"I did have to go to Chagrin Falls three times this week to convince a client that the huge Turner Topiary we imported from England was right for her foyer. I did it, though." She smiled with satisfaction and glanced at the Regulator wall clock.

"Oh, oh, look at the time. I'll have to run up and give Paul a nudge."

As if on cue, Paul appeared, wearing blue jeans and a tattered red stained shirt. He hadn't spent much time on his costume, but he looked menacing and mean when he slipped an incredibly ugly mask over his handsome face.

"Where's Sweets?" Jamie screamed! "Where's Sweets?"

Sweets was Liz's pet name for her husband and Jamie had called him that since he'd been able to pronounce it.

Paul tore the mask from his face and took Jamie from his high chair.

"See, it's Daddy, Jamie. It's Sweets. Don't be afraid, honey," Liz said soothingly.

They both cuddled him for a long time, then Paul straddled him on his shoulders and galloped around the kitchen and down the hall neighing like a horse. By the time Paul got to the front door, Jamie was giggling and Liz had taken their coats from the hall closet.

"Mommie and I have to go now, Jamie. You be good for Nana."

Paul and Liz drove away smiling and blowing kisses until they were out of sight. It was wonderful to see them going out for a good time. They both looked as though they needed a vacation. Paul had lost a lot of weight lately and they had been working long grueling hours.

I left the porch light on, and Jamie and I went upstairs to his room. He proudly showed me everything in it, from the antique rocker Liz had found at an flea market to the many stuffed monkeys Paul had collected for him. Jabbering happily, he gave each one to me to inspect and kiss.

He hadn't objected when I washed his hair at bathtime as he usually did. His hair is blond and very curly, just like Paul's. It curls more tightly when it's wet so I didn't try to brush it for fear I'd pull it and make him cry. I wanted the day to end as happily as it had begun so I toweled it dry and put him in his blue pajamas with the monkey applique on the front.

"Time for bed," I said as I swung him high into the air and into his crib.

"Sing, Nana, sing!" he giggled, clapping his pudgy little hands together. I have an awful voice, but my grandson can listen to me for hours. After a couple of choruses of BROTHER JOHN and PLAYMATE his eyes grew heavy and closed, long silky lashes touching his cheeks.

I covered him snugly, kissed him gently and stood there for a long time thinking how lucky I was to have a beautiful grandson. I tiptoed out of his room and went downstairs, thankful that the long day was ending. I went into the darkened living room, plopped into a big overstuffed chair and hoisted my feet onto the matching ottoman.

"Granny," I said to myself, "you are getting long in the tooth."

I rested my head on the back of the chair and watched the light from the street lamps shining through the lace curtains make an intricately patterned kaleidoscope on the ceiling. It had such a hypnotic effect that in no time I was asleep.

I was awakened by the shuddering crash of the front door slamming.

"You will not call a cab, bitch. I'll take your stupid mother home!"

I snapped fully awake and realized with astonishment that it was Paul's voice I heard.

"Please keep your voice down, Paul. You'll wake the baby."

"The baby, the baby," Paul simpered, mimicking Liz. "Always the good little mother. Can't stay up late anymore. Have to get up early to get to work to make out with the boss!"

"Paul, for God's sake, Mom will hear you--"

"Shut up, slut," he growled. "You have no energy when you're with me. Who are you saving your energy for--"

"Stop it *now*, Paul!" She tried to outshout him but his voice rose to a scream and his language grew disgusting as he raged on.

I was stunned and horror-stricken but couldn't just sit there, an unwitting eavesdropper, so I went into the hall.

When Paul saw me, a transformation took place, like a dissolve in a horror movie. One minute he stood before me, his body rigid, lips curled in a sneer more frightening than the gaping snarl on the mask he had worn to the Halloween party. The next, his body seemed to wilt. His shoulders dropped, the ugly grimace slackened and the glowering monster melted away. All the life seemed to leave him. He turned away from us, eyes downcast, and went quietly up the stairs.

Liz stood there, wet mascara cutting muddy rivulets through the rouge on her cheeks, and watched until he reached the top of the stairs and disappeared in the darkened upper hall. All I could do was hold her and cry.

"What happened to Paul?"

"Coke, Mom, cocaine," she said wearily and slumped down onto the settee by the front door.

At the time I knew nothing about drug abuse, but I knew that the well ordered world that I had believed my family lived in had just fallen apart.

"Has he ever hit you?" I asked, dreading the answer.

"No, Mom, he never has," she said calmly and rose from the bench.

"You'd better go home now. I'll call a cab. Don't worry, I'll be all right."

I remembered being surprised at how quickly she had recovered from Paul's verbal assault until I realized with a jolt that she had been through this scene many times before.

That was six months ago. Paul refused to see a therapist or go to a drug rehabilitation center. He steadfastly denied he had a drug problem. He was a stockbroker, and he insisted that when the pressures of his job let up he would be all right. Of course, the pressures of his job never let up, and one night he hit Liz. Afraid that it was just a question of time before he hit Jamie, she moved out and was quickly divorced. She was seeing a therapist and starting to accept the facts about addiction.

Liz suggested that Dan and I see one, too, or join a self-help group, but we hadn't thought it necessary. So here I sat in my strawberry kitchen, still unable to believe that cocaine had become the most important thing in Paul's life. Paul, who had been like a son to me.

Suddenly, I realized how foolish I was to think that Paul's addiction would not affect me and all of us profoundly! How could I think that hiding in my kitchen day after day, waiting for the pain to lessen was ever going to make me feel better? Shouldn't I accept that there were going to be many moments like the one today when I run into

Sue at the supermarket? And last week, when I baby sat for Liz.

At naptime I had told Jamie to get his favorite toy to take to bed with him. He went directly to his monkey collection and picked out a brand new one. Paul had brought it to him on one of his infrequent visits.

"Look, Nana, look at Monkey Face. That's his name," Jamie said as he shook the monkey furiously, making two blacks dots in its glass eyes spin crazily.

"See, he rolls his eyes!" he said, laughing. Then, abruptly, he stopped laughing and shaking the monkey. He hugged it close. "Sweets brought this to me," he said. "You 'member Sweets, don't you, Nana?"

HELEN ON WHEELS

"I've been up here for forty-five years and I still can't spend every minute on Cloud Nine. Everyone else in my family spends all their time over there playing bridge. But here I am, worrying about Helen again." Zola sat down, adjusted her wings, and pushed aside some scudding clouds which were obstructing her view of Madison, Wisconsin.

"Now watch, Peter, here she comes."

St. Peter looked down on a halcyon summer day, and saw a woman on a small grey and black electric scooter tool her way out of her apartment building and head toward the corner of Hancock and Gorham Streets.

"I think Helen looks very well," he said. "Look, she's smiling."

"Well, of course she's smiling. That's her devilish smile." Zola smiled knowingly. "Ever since she discovered that the stretch of sidewalk between Hancock and Johnson is nearly always deserted, she thinks it's her personal Indy 500 tract. Just watch..."

Helen reached the corner, took a last loving look at the view of Lake Mendota across Gorham Street, and nosed her scooter around the corner, where she stopped. She checked the sidewalk on Hancock for pedestrians, then turned the knob on the small black box attached to the handle of her scooter up to six, the maximum speed the little machine could reach, and then pushed the starter release. For some reason, she thought about her mother as she sailed down the sidewalk at full throttle, her hair and skirt ruffling in the cool summer breeze. She felt wonderful!

"You see, Peter! She's sixty-five years old, and lame, and she is still a tomboy!" Zola brushed away a tear that had formed when she said the word "lame", watched her daughter slow down, cross Johnson Street and disappear beneath a roof of thick green maple leaves.

"Come on, Zola, she hasn't been this happy for a long time. That little scooter has opened a whole new world for her. She's just enjoying the independence that little machine gives her."

St Peter helped the plump middle-aged angel to her feet. "She's probably a lot like you." He patted her hand. "I've seen you running wildly, back and forth through the stardust, scattering it all over the place. You know, the child in all of us never dies, thank Heaven."

Zola smiled sheepishly. "That's true," she said as she and Peter bounced along on cottony fluff. "I just hope she doesn't hurt herself. She has made a new friend who has a scooter like hers. The next thing you know, they'll be drag racing."

Peter sighed deeply and shook his head. "Honestly, Zola, I'd report you to your Higher Power if I thought it would make you stop worrying about your daughter, but I know it won't do any good. He has more complaints about your kind of behavior than even he can

handle.   All   the   mothers   up   here   are   just
like you."

TWICE IN A LIFETIME

I, Susan O'Hare, *will* go to that Botox party tonight. I made up my mind as I was checking my make-up in the three-way mirror which was attached to the nineteen-thirties' dresser I had acquired at a private antique sale. I was shocked to see the deep lines between my eyebrows. The lines on my forehead had deepened since I last took a good look at my face.

Why should I be surprised? I had spent every spare minute on a tennis court with John from the day we married until he died two years ago. Every other spare minute I spent in my garden--yes--in the sun, of course.

Damn it, I still have a good figure and I'm sixty years old. I'm not supposed to look twenty. Besides, John liked the way I look. Tears filled my eyes.

"He's no longer here, Susan," I said to the lady in the mirror. I stared at my aging image.

"You are lonesome, so lonesome," I whispered to myself.

I wiped the useless tears from my eyes and finished getting ready. At least it will be a new experience.

Polly Ashberry, my best friend, picked me up at seven-thirty. She had been my best friend since college. Because of her I had an exceptional college experience. She had the most outgoing personality and the zaniest sense of humor of anyone I had ever known.

27

Everyone loved Polly. She had introduced me to John.

When Polly mentioned the Botox party I thought she was joking. It would be just like her to make up something like that, but, alas we were going to a real Botox party tonight.

As we drove along Lakeshore Drive, I looked at her perfect profile and asked, "Why are we going, Polly, you just had your face done a while back?"

"It's *the* thing to do." She looked over at me, eyebrows arched high, looking down her small nose in her V.I.P. pose.

"And, of course, *the* Polly Ashberry always does *the* thing to do, darling."

We laughed so hard other drivers stared at us as they passed by.

"The food is worth going for. Jane Sutton has one of the best cooks on the North Shore. A real chef. Of course, you have the best cook," I said as we pulled into the long tree-lined driveway which led to Jane's mansion. It was a grey stone castle. All it needed were a few gargoyles to make you think you were living in Medieval times.

"How can Jane and Bob live in this spooky-looking place?" Polly asked.

"Probably because it was given to them by Bob's parents," I said sarcastically. "I have to admit it does have all manner of beautiful touches inside. Irreplaceable mosaic tiles and the Romanesque windows are to die for."

"I know that's true," Polly said, "so let's go in and check out the artifacts and eat."

The food and wine were delicious as expected. Polly and I mingled and chatted with the other guests. Almost all knew each other from the country club we belonged to. All of them were giddy with anticipation about this unusual event.

Finally, Jane clapped for silence. She had a tall distinguished-looking man in tow and it took a few minutes for the large room of hyper women to settle down. Jane introduced the famous Dr. Ira Schulman, and offered herself as an example of the use of Botox. The frown lines were gone and her forehead was as smooth as a baby's behind.

Dr. Schulman, the renowned plastic surgeon, gave us a short history of the use of Botox, and explained how simple it was to inject it into the face and that the wrinkles would be gone between one and three days. Discomfort almost none. He offered to give the injections tonight if we chose to get one, told us the price, and asked for questions.

"Is it true that Botox has been known to somehow go wrong and disfigure the eye?" Mary Lou Dayton wanted to know.

"It has happened. I know of only one case in the hundreds of cases I have handled, but I was able to correct this with surgery."

"Dr. Schulman, how long will the effects of one injection last? Does it last forever?" Beautiful Polly had asked the question. She had asked for me because she knew I wouldn't ask any questions.

"For most, about six months." He smiled familiarly at Polly. He had done her face two years before.

I would have done it, if I wasn't so terrified of needles. No. I wouldn't. I have faced the fact that I am sixty years old and can't look like a young girl forever.

I wished with all my heart I could look like a young girl when I first saw Martin Gardner at a lunch at Polly's. He was standing on the patio talking to Ken, Polly's husband. He reminded me so much of my John! His hands were thrust in the pockets of his beige linen slacks and he rocked gently back and forth on his heels as John used to do and his hair was snow white, like John's!

He took my breath away! When I got closer to him I saw that this man looked very much like Cary Grant, his skin was darkly tanned and he had a deep cleft in his chin. Even my John couldn't compare to Cary Grant.

Well, Polly had done it again. She'd found a new man for me, as if this guy couldn't have any woman he wanted. I bet he would want to kill Polly and Ken when he met me. I was very wrong.

It was a rare, beautiful and warm day on the North Shore for April. We ate on the patio of Polly and Ken's ultra modern mansion on the shore of Lake Michigan. From the moment Martin and I met we felt we had known each

other forever. He had played tenni
life, and in spite of that he was a
player, as I was. Everyone made jokes ab
our lack of expertise on the courts. The
jokes weren't that funny but Martin and I
laughed our heads off while Polly and Ken
looked knowingly at each other.

Martin and I made a tennis date for the
very next day at the country club and that
was the beginning of our romance.

Martin never seemed to notice or care
about my wrinkled brow. We were always
together except for when he and Ken were out
of town on business. At those times I was so
lonesome for him I thought I might die before
he came back. All I could do was work in my
garden and moon about the night in May when
Martin took me in his arms and told me he
loved me. He had asked me to marry him that
night and I hadn't hesitated to say yes.

Ken and Martin had a lot in common.
They owned real estate all over the world and
had their fingers in many pies.

They were now involved in a big
operation in Florida. Martin had bought a
lot on Collins Avenue in Miami and had begun
to construct a four hundred and forty unit
condo luxury hi-rise. They had built and
furnished models for buyers to see before
purchasing a unit. They had already sold
half of the building before it was even
built. Ken and Martin had taken care of all
this while the other two partners sat back
and waited for the profits to roll in.

Polly, Ken, Martin and I were having dinner at my house the Wednesday before Ken and Martin were to leave for Miami. They would only be gone a few days, but I was already dreading it.

I suppose I was afraid Martin would find someone else. Everyone he knew except me on the North Shore was very, very rich, and he was very, very handsome. Their homes were sumptuous compared to the large, Queen Anne painted lady with the beautiful garden that was my home. I loved it dearly. When John and I bought the house it needed a lot of work and the garden was very sorry-looking. We owned an upscale antique store and John was an architectural landscaper. Together we had made our home a gem. We never envied our more well-heeled friends and neighbors and we felt right at home in Winnetka.

When we finished dinner and went into the living room to have coffee and port, we left behind the dining room with its Duncan Phyfe furniture for the lady I'd hired for the night to clean.

"I'm afraid we have to leave early, Susan," Polly said. She set her cup on the cocktail table and stood. "I'm leaving early, too, for New Orleans to see Mom while Ken is away."

"Martin, don't stay too long, buddy," Ken said. "We have to leave early, too."

Martin stood by me with his arm squeezing my waist, and a sly grin on his face. "Pretty soon I won't be leaving at all. Her engagement ring is being sized at

Tiffany's in Chicago. She'll be wearing it by next week."

"It's so beautiful!" I sighed.

"I'm so happy for you," Polly said, and hugged me tightly before she and Ken left.

When they were gone we sat on the couch, sipped our port and petted like teenagers.

"I better go before I can't go," Martin said. "I could be back by Sunday and we can take up where we left off here."

On Saturday I was pinching dead heads off the petunias in my garden, thinking that I may get married in late August in my own garden. If John knew how happy I am, he'd be very happy for me. He'd be pleased his work on the garden meant so much to me.

A shadow fell over me. I turned quickly, looked up to find Ken standing behind me.

"Ken, why are you back so soon? Where's Martin?"

My heartbeats began to speed up. I stood up quickly, almost eye to eye with Ken. He opened his mouth to speak, closed it, and stood there as if he could not speak. He began to shake.

I grabbed his arms. "Is Martin alright?" I screamed. "Has there been an accident?" Tears spilled down my cheeks at the thought.

Then I started shaking. Ken seemed to wake from a dream. "No, no accident," he mumbled. "When I got to the airport, Martin had left a message for me saying he would be later flying to Miami--for me to go on." He paused as if he couldn't go on.

"Martin would be there later and explain." He stopped speaking again and looked down at his shoes.

I gave him time to collect himself. Finally, he was able to continue. "At the hotel there was another message. It said that he and Polly had taken all the money from the project and gone away together and that we would never see them again." Ken broke into tears.

"Oh, my God! It can't be true!" I was too shocked to cry. I couldn't seem to understand what he had said to me.

This had to be a nightmare--yes--I would wake up soon!

Ken reached out for me and put his arms around me. We stood this way for a long time. Two people trying to survive a shock like a physical blow.

I got hold of myself, stopped shaking, but began to cry again.

"Martin didn't show up at the scheduled meeting and left the partners no messages. As for Polly..." He walked to the garden bench. He dropped into it like a stone, started to say something but couldn't. He covered his face with his hands. I sat next to him before I fell. My legs were so weak, they had begun to buckle.

He looked at me and said, "As for Polly, she never went to her mother's, she wasn't even expected."

"How could they do this to us? Martin and I were planning our wedding!"

"Susan, we have to face it, Martin is a big time con artist. He conned me and our friends who are in on the project. Polly isn't too bad at the con game herself."

"Why would Polly do this to me? We've been life long friends."

"Yes, but you really never knew Polly. This isn't her first affair, Susan. I put up with it because I've loved her since we were all in college.

"Polly loves excitement and money. She knew John had left you a lot of insurance money. If the partners and I hadn't had as much money as we needed, there was always you. Polly had reminded me." He paused abruptly and searched my face. I felt an actual physical pain in my heart.

"You didn't give him money, did you Susan?"

He needn't have asked. I knew he could tell the answer by looking at my stricken face. The face that Botox had never touched.

I put both hands over my critically injured heart and laughed...and laughed...and laughed.

THE MAGIC ROOM

My mother's brother was the only artist in our family, as far as I know. He was talented, but sadly, he was also unsuccessful and alcoholic. Needless to say, my family would not have considered him a likely role model, but actually he was.

My uncle lived with my grandparents, and had a tiny studio atop the old garage in the back of their house.

The garage was built like a barn, which it undoubtedly had been at one time. It was sturdy but old, its wood weathered to a silvery sheen like the barns that often dot a country landscape. My uncle's studio was a small space, about six feet by eight feet, in what was once a loft, and to me, it was truly a magic place.

My uncle supplied me with huge pieces of paper from gigantic pads, nothing like the 9 x 13 construction paper I had at home. He let me use his charcoal and water colors. I was too young for oil paints and he, himself, used expensive pastels sparingly. We were in the depths of the Depression and those art supplies must have been a real luxury. I can still smell the sharp aroma of turpentine and the faint indescribable essence of colored chalk powder when I think of that wonderful room.

There is one thing I'll always be grateful to my uncle for. He showed me how to really look at things--not to see just a fat black crow but to appreciate the bluish iridescent sheen on the top of his head.

Sometimes in the middle of a dinner when the sun was setting, he would get up from the table, take my hand, lead me outside and say, "Come, you *have* to see this."

My uncle did what a lot of young men did during the Depression. He went west. He got a job in an aircraft factory in California and never painted again, but he did stop drinking.

I, on the other hand, have never stopped doing artwork. I have nothing hanging in the Louvre, but I have worked for two major potteries, represented American Crayon Company in Louisville, Cleveland and New York. For that company I demonstrated and taught china painting and textile painting.

I married an artist who has had a successful career in advertising, and shown his painting and sculptures in art galleries.

We have three children and when the first was born, I looked into his tiny pink face and knew I would never work outside the home again. I would never leave him in the care of someone else if I could help it.

I have never regretted that decision, because now that I am a grandmother, I have had the privilege of taking two generations of children by their hands, leading them outside at sunset and saying to them, "Come, you *have* to see this."

JULIE

Tim didn't like Jack Barnes. So why was he here? It was one thing to help a guy move, but to deliver stuff to his ex-wife was something else.

"Face it, jerk, he's your boss and he helped you find an apartment when you came to Chicago." Tim said this out loud to an empty elevator as it shot up to the 40th floor of the Gold Coast apartment building.

His ears were popping like firecrackers when he stepped out of the elevator. He looked to his right, where Jack Barnes stood by the doorway of his apartment.

"Jesus, I hate moving!" Jack said when Tim reached 40A. "I hope this is the last move I make in a long, long time."

They stepped inside, went directly to the living room and into the lap of luxury. The view of Lake Michigan outside an entire wall of glass took Tim's breath away.

"Why would you ever give this up?" Tim gasped.

"Nothing but bad memories...the last days before Julie left...you know." There wasn't a trace of emotion in Jack's voice. "Come to the kitchen and have some coffee."

Tim followed Jack into a state-of-the-art kitchen and sat on a high stool while Jack poured coffee from a fancy plunger-style pot.

"Ground the beans myself from a special blend," Jack said proudly.

Tim reached for the sugar.

"You wouldn't put sugar in this coffee!" Jack exclaimed with more feeling for the coffee than he had expressed for the end of his marriage.

Tim drew his hand back from the sugar bowl like a small boy caught reaching for the cookie jar.

"Julie used to load her coffee with sugar. It made me crazy. This coffee should be savored--like good wine.

"Are you sure Julie won't mind a stranger bringing her things to her?"

"Not at all! She'll probably invite you in for lunch. Our divorce wasn't hostile. We both realized we had married too young. Right out of college, in fact."

For a brief moment Tim saw what might have passed as a flicker of fond remembrance in Jack's eyes.

"Let's face it, I outgrew Julie." Jack slid off his stool. "Bring your coffee and let's go to the bedroom. I haven't finished packing her trunk."

The bedroom was even more spectacular than the living room. A tableau of Lake Michigan was reflected in mirrored panels opposite still another windowed wall. A huge custom bed seemed to float in the midst of vast reaches of sky and water.

"I've never seen anything like this!" Tim whistled. "It must be hard to give this up. Of course, I know the rent must be out of sight without Julie's income."

Jack couldn't have looked more wounded if Tim had punched him in the gut.

"I'm moving to a larger apartment. I don't need Julie's paltry salary." His face caught fire as if the ascot he had tucked in the neck of his shirt was choking him. "I'd have been happy if Julie had stopped working! Then, maybe she would have had time for me and the things I like to do--need to do to get ahead."

Jack walked into a closet as big as Tim's bedroom and grabbed a silver framed photograph off a shelf and handed it to Tim. "You wouldn't think by looking at her that she would be iron-willed and stubborn as a mule, would you?"

Tim saw a pixie-faced girl with short red curls and bright blue eyes smiling squarely into the camera. To Tim she looked more confident than stubborn.

"What does she do?" Tim asked with real interest, unable to take his eyes off Julie's pert physiognomy.

"She teaches Special Ed.," Jack said and came out of the closet again carrying a plump patchwork quilt. "Look at this. Julie's grandmother made this, and she would have put *this* quilt on *that* bed if I hadn't stopped her." He went back into the closet and brought out a shoebox, opened it and pulled out a pair of plain wornout tennis shoes.

"Now these were the straws that broke the camel's back." Jack squeezed the little shoes so tightly his knuckles nearly popped through his skin. "Julie was supposed to meet Jeffery Hines, his wife and me for dinner one night. You know Jeffery...he's the governor's liaison to the agency...you worked with him on that Illinois tourism thing we did, didn't you?"

Tim nodded, half listening, still drawn to the girl's face in the photograph. She reminded him of his kid sister back in Vermont. Thoughts of home came to mind and lightly touched his heart. Winter days when he wrote stories in his little room tucked away under a sloping snow-covered roof while his sister taught A B Cs to her dolls lined up on the stairs outside his door.

"Anyway, Julie and Jeffery's wife were supposed to meet us at my club after our handball game. We were in the bar waiting for the girls. Jeffery's wife shows up dressed to kill. Designer clothes head to toe." Jack shook his head in disgust. "In comes Julie, late of course, she had been on a field trip to Lamb's Farm with her class, way the hell out in the boonies. *She* was L. L. Bean all the way." Jack threw the sneakers into the trunk. "And these God damned stupid shoes topped off her outfit."

"She must really love kids! How come you didn't have any in eight years?" Tim regretted his question the minute it was out of his mouth and he saw little veins twitching at the corner of Jack's eye. "Sorry, Jack, I shouldn't have asked such a personal question."

"It's okay." Jack straightened his ascot and composed himself. "I get madder than hell when I think about all the fights we had about having kids." He was quiet for a moment. "We both agreed we wouldn't have children until our careers were well established. We hadn't been married three years when she wanted to have a baby. Christ, the last year we were married I thought I'd jump out of the window if she mentioned her biological clock just one more time." Jack took Julie's picture out of Tim's hand and slammed it into the trunk.

"Funny, isn't it, just when I'd reached my goal and the time was right, we split."

"You know," Jack continued, "she could have been anything she wanted to be. She graduated Summa Cum Laude from Vassar. What does she do? She chooses a career in education, the lowest God damned paying profession she could have chosen." With that he shut the lid of the old wallpapered trunk on all that was left of an eight year marriage.

When Tim came, he had planned to tell Jack his reasons for going to a writer's seminar in Madison where Julie was living, but he knew now he wouldn't. His dream since college was to earn enough money to quit writing advertising copy and start writing fiction full time. He was now certain that Jack would not understand him any more than he had understood his wife.

Jack checked his Rolex and went to the phone.

"I've got a handball game in an hour. I'll call the doorman to come up and help you get the trunk to the car."

"Don't get the doorman, I can manage this myself."

Suddenly, Tim had to get out of that apartment. "I've got to go, too, Jack, or I'm going to be late myself." He hoisted the little trunk easily onto his shoulder and headed for the front door.

Jack reached the door ahead of Tim and held it open.

"It's good to see you polishing your skills." Jack patted Tim's shoulder. "You keep it up and you'll be Assistant Creative Director very soon. And thanks again for taking this stuff to her. God knows what she wants with it, but if I know Julie she'll probably wear those fucking tennis shoes again."

"See you Monday," Tim called over his shoulder as he made a beeline for the elevator. He was anxious to get to Madison. He didn't want to be late for the seminar, but more than that he was anxious to meet Julie Barnes. In fact he could hardly wait to meet her.

A.J. KELLY - About The Author

A.J. thinks of herself as a Southern writer, having spent her formative years in Kentucky. Her stories are filled with colorful characters and situations. She now lives in Chicago. Her husband of thirty-eight years was the late David Romaine Bohme, noted violinist and conductor.

TROPHIES

He was like a boat with barnacles, scars and bruises all over his body from pulling in fish. His face testified to days in the sun and salt air--dark and craggy.

"You're late," Captain Sam said.

"Yeah, I know," Sweeney growled, dropping his duffel bag on the deck of the boat.

"That drinking is goin' a get you."

"Who gives a shit," Sweeney replied.

He didn't feel like arguing with Captain Sam. His head throbbed from a night of drinking. He had never told Captain Sam anything about his private life, how he came to Marathon Key. It was after his eight-year-old daughter Laney had been killed by a hit-and-run driver. The day he buried her, just hours after the funeral, he threw some clothes into his pickup and started driving, not knowing where he was heading. He ended up in Marathon. When his money ran out, he ended up with Captain Sam.

Just then, three people came on board for a day of fishing-- a man, a woman, and a little girl about Laney's age.

Don't go there, he told himself.

After the run was over, Sweeney went to the Outrigger Bar, sitting in his usual dark corner. He saw a couple at the bar. The man was very loud. Must be telling off-color jokes to the bartender, Sweeney thought. The three of them were laughing hysterically.

47

Through his haze Sweeney recognized the woman's laughter. Only one woman laughs like that, he thought.

She walked over to the jukebox and fumbled in her purse for change. She brought out a bill. Turning toward Sweeney, she said, "Do you have change for a dollar?"

Sweeney stuck a hand in his pocket, came up with quarters.

She looked at him, then came closer. She looked again. "Sweeney, is that you?" She pulled the fisherman's hat back off his forehead.

"It is you," she said. "Of all the people to run into. What are you doing here?"

Sweeney felt his face tighten. "What does it look like? I'm drinking," he answered.

"No, I mean here, in Marathon."

"I live here."

"Since when, Sweeney?"

Before he could answer, the man at the bar, the loud one, yelled, "Hey, Madeline, what's keeping you so long?"

She yelled back, "I ran into an old friend, Frank." Then quietly to Sweeney, she said, "That's my husband."

Frank got off his barstool and came over to them, carrying his drink.

"Would you believe who I found?" she asked.

"Who?" Frank asked, looking at Sweeney through half-closed eyes.

"My ex. You know. Sweeney," she said.

"Yeah? So, what do you do here, Sweeney?" Frank asked.

"I work on a fishing boat."

"In other words, you're a flunkie," Frank said with a smirk.

"C'mon, Frank," Madeline said. "Stop that."

Sweeney looked away, wishing he wasn't hearing this. He felt tired now, wanted to get away from them.

"Frank, didn't you say we needed someone to take us out deep-sea fishing?" Madeline asked. "Maybe Sweeney can take us."

Frank didn't look too happy with that suggestion, but Madeline insisted.

"You two work it out," Sweeney said. "The boat's at the end of the pier. Just ask for Captain Sam."

That night Sweeney had a hard time sleeping. He thought about Madeline, how warm and soft her body had been. I don't blame her for leaving, he thought. She was so young, only seventeen, and wanted things I couldn't give her on a housepainter's pay. She couldn't cope with a new baby: Laney was colicky for so long. I could forgive her for all that. But I can't forgive her for not showing up for Laney's funeral.

The next morning Sweeney arose early. He showered, and shaved off his week's growth of beard. He shampooed his sun-streaked hair and pulled it back in a ponytail.

"Not bad for an old bastard like you," he said, looking into the mirror. But he felt like a plucked chicken.

It was a beautiful morning. The sun cast its light on the water, making it look like a thousand dancing diamonds. Pelicans perched on the decaying posts. They were diving for their breakfast, bringing up fish in their spoon bills.

Sweeney saw Madeline and Frank coming up the gangplank. Madeline bounced in front, her chestnut hair waving in the wind.

Frank was having trouble balancing. His heavy body swayed from side to side. He stopped to wipe the sweat from his forehead, breathing hard. He saw Sweeney looking at him and snarled, "What are you gawkin' at? Let's get this tub under way."

Sweeney knew he was going to have a hard time with Frank.

"Oh, look at the pretty pelicans," Madeline said.

"Ugliest bird I ever saw," Frank growled.

After they were under way Sweeney decided to keep himself busy, so he went about setting the rigs and dumping bait into one of the holding tanks.

Madeline went below to change into her bathing suit. When she returned she was wearing a shimmering white, two-piece thing. Sweeney tried not to look at her, but couldn't resist a few sidelong glances. She still has a good body, he thought.

Frank fell into one of the white : chairs. Madeline went on top of the hatcn to sun herself.

"If you want, I'll loosen the reel and you can troll on the way out," Sweeney said.

"Yeah, do that," Frank answered. "I just hope you know where the damn fish are."

"Fishing's not a perfect science," Sweeney said. "Sometimes you catch, sometimes you don't."

"Well, I sure as hell better catch with the price I'm paying."

The morning was uneventful. Not a nibble. Frank continued to grouch. But that afternoon Frank's line began to tug and pull, and the reel made a zinging sound.

"You've got a big fish there," Sweeney said. "Don't try to horse him in. Play 'em. Play 'em. Let out more line. Give him room to run."

Frank played the fish for almost an hour. Finally he said to Sweeney, "You take it. My arms feel like they're comin' off."

Sweeney took the line and worked it. The fish broke the water, spinning like a ballet dancer.

"Will you look at that," Frank said. "It's a sail."

Its colors were blue and turquoise. It looked as if it were glowing inside-- fluorescent.

"Here, I'll take it now," Frank yelled.

"It's not ready to come in yet, Frank."

"Don't tell me how to catch a fish. I been catchin' 'em for forty years."

Finally the fish got tired out and began to come closer to the boat. It broke the water one more time. It took Captain Sam, Sweeney, and Frank to pull it into the boat. Sweeney tapped it lightly on the head, just enough to stun it, and put it in the other holding tank.

"Let's head in," Frank said. "I'm tired out. My arms are killing me. Besides, I want to show off my fish." He looked to the hatch, and screamed, "Hey, Madeline, did you see what I caught? C'mon down here."

As she came down, Sweeney said, "Watch out, Madeline, it can fin you."

"Oh, how beautiful," she said. "But you're gonna let it go, aren't you, Frank?"

"Hell, no. It's probably the biggest fish caught this season. And you want me to let it go? That sucker's going over the fireplace in the den."

When they reached the pier, the three men carried it off the boat.

"Help me get it over to the display board," Frank shouted.

Madeline walked very fast behind them.

The display board had heavy spikes driven in from the backside. Frank lifted the fish and started for the board. Madeline began to pull at his arm.

"Don't do it, Frank," she cried. "It's still alive. I know it is. And it's so beautiful, it deserves to live. Put in the water, Frank, please."

Frank raised the fish and slammed it onto the sharp spikes. You could hear the sound of tearing flesh.

Madeline began to hit Frank. "You bastard," she cried. "Are you satisfied now?"

"You crazy woman. Leave me alone." At that, Frank began to walk toward the bar. "I need a drink."

Madeline fell to the foot of the display board. She was crying bitterly now. The blood was running down the fish's body and onto the ground. Little by little it began to lose its brilliant colors, finally turning a dull, metallic grey.

Sweeney had been watching Madeline and stopped swabbing the deck of the boat. He came down and walked to her.

She was still crying. "Why did he do it? Why?"

"Some men fish for fun. Some men fish for trophies," Sweeney said.

Madeline looked up at him. "I'm sorry, Sweeney. I'm sorry for everything. For leaving you, Sweeney. I guess I was blinded by Frank's money. I've never been happy with him." She paused for a few seconds. "God, he treats me like one of his trophies. And most of all, I was such a coward by not coming to Laney's funeral. I felt so guilty about leaving her."

Sweeney felt sorry for her. He pulled her up off the ground. "C'mon, Madeline, let's go for a walk."

"I'm leaving him Sweeney, and with my settlement I'm coming back here, and buying a small house. And a fishing boat."

Sweeney knew where she was going with this, and started to walk away from her.

"I'll need a captain," she yelled after him. "Are you gonna be around?"

He stopped, then turned, but didn't speak.

She asked again, "Well, are you gonna be around?"

"I don't know," Sweeney answered.

"Think about it," she said.

That night Sweeney stayed on the boat. He slept under the stars. He remembered when he and Madeline went on a camping trip to Arkansas. They, too, slept under the stars, huddling together to keep warm.

God, what went wrong? Was it as much my fault? How could I ever trust her again?

The next morning Madeline was at the boat bright and early.

"Well, did you think about what I said?"

"Ye--ah."

"And what did you decide? Are you going to be around?"

Sweeney sighed, then took a deep breath. "Yeah, I'll be around."

DRIED FLOWERS

Mama had been reading poetry all morning. For days she had played the piano and sung love songs... "Promise me that someday you and I will take our love together to some sky." She did this when my father was away. He was a veterinarian and traveled extensively for the County. He wore jodhpurs and colorful shirts. The women loved him, and he loved the women.

I sat quietly in the corner, reading my movie magazine. I knew it wouldn't be long now.

"How would you like to go to Harlan?" she asked.

There it was. She was going to Serena's.

Serena was a fortune teller in the next town. I had heard Mama and Nettie, the black woman that worked for my Aunt Olivia, talking in hushed whispers about Serena. Mama had never taken me there. Now she was letting me in on her secret. I must be growing up, I thought.

I looked at her sitting next to me on the bus. How beautiful she was in her navy blue flowered dress with the lace collar. Her yellow straw hat shading her soft hazel eyes and delicate face. She hummed softly as we watched the passing scenery. The cliffs where in winter, icicles formed like ice palaces, and I imagined a pale princess held captive by a handsome prince.

55

We passed mining camps where bare-bottomed children played in the muddy lanes. "That's what you'll get if you're not careful," she said. I knew better, I was going to Hollywood and become a movie star. "Children are nice," she continued, "but they ruin you figger. I had the best one in town, everybody thought so."

We were coming to the outskirts of town, where black people lived in shacks precariously hanging over the river on wooden stilts. My father told me that once fish were plentiful here, but now a scum of coal dust floated on top, and no fish had been seen there for years.

When we got to the middle of town, the afternoon sun was casting long shadows on the walls and Greek columns of the Court House. Old men in white Panama hats were congregated under the willow trees, spitting tobacco juice in the yellowing summer grass. We passed Skidmore's Funeral Home. Mama turned in her seat to look at it. A reverent look came over her face. She loved funerals. She went to every one, regardless of whether or not she knew the deceased. She took flowers from their wreaths and pressed them in our family Bible. I found them years later, dried and crumbling, and asked her whose they were. She never remembered.

Once she took me to see a man who'd been shot by a jealous wife. The room was bathed in a dim golden light. There was the overpowering smell of flowers, the sound of faint organ music. The man's face was bloated and bulged over his collar. His lips were a sickly blue. An old woman in a Spanish shawl said, "Don't he look natural." Natural, I thought, he's dead.

We passed Main Street and then Mound Street. Young boys flirted with passing, giggly girls. As we went by the doughnut factory, I could detect the aroma of sugar and pungent yeast.

"When we get to the bus station, we'll go in back so no one sees us," she said.

We had to make our way down a back street and across the railroad tracks. The houses here were long, shot-gun style, stretched out on an unpaved muddy road. It was a hot day and the doors of most of the houses were open. Serena's was closed. Mama knocked several times before she answered.

Serena was short and fat, with a round face and high cheekbones. She wore a black and red scarf tied around her head. I stared at her, for Mama had said she was a hundred percent American Indian. I'd never seen an Indian before. She and Mama talked in whispers. Then Serena took her in the back room, telling me to wait.

The room was bare with the exception of a couch with the springs pushing through the cushions, a chair with the stuffings coming out of it, and a picture on the wall showing a red heart with sparks emanating from it. Looking at it, I prayed, "Please God, don't let some jealous man shoot my father...and don't let Serena tell Mama anything bad."

When Mama came out, she was all smiles. Giddy as a school girl. "Wait 'til I tell you what Serena said," she told me.

But she waited until we were back in the heart of town and sitting in Ackley's Cafe. She ordered hot dogs for both of us, and then she began. "We have to clean up the house real good, 'cause Serena said we're goin' to have some unexpected company."

I hoped it wouldn't be my Aunt Mabel from Benson, with my cousin, Lorelei. I envied her black curly hair and blue eyes. My hair was the color of straw and just as straight.

"We're goin' to get a letter from an unknown person," she went on, "and some money from an undisclosed source. Then I'll buy you that coat you've had your eye on in Fuller's Store."

My enthusiasm began to rise as high as Mama's.

"Best of all," she whispered, "Serena said your daddy's not seeing any women anymore." She went on excitedly, her eyes beaming. "We have to go to Woolworth's. I want to buy some potholders and dishtowels. Then we have to go to Piggly-Wiggly's so I can get pineapple in syrup for an upside down cake, and we need freshly ground coffee, too."

I could already smell the nutty-burnt coffee beans. I found myself getting more caught up in Mama's excitement.

At Woolworth's she gave me a dollar and told me to get whatever I wanted. I bought

"Gone with the Wind" paper dolls. Later I played with them under my bed, in my own little world. Then Mama tried on lipsticks and asked me which one looked the best. I told her the pink one looked the best, but she took the reddest one in the bunch.

"I'll treat you to an ice cream sundae," she said, "if you promise not to tell your grandma I went to Serena's."

I wasn't going to tell Grandma. I didn't want her to yell at Mama the way she did when they'd sit in the swing on our front porch and talk about my father.

"That's what killed your daddy," Grandma would say to her. "You so young and all. He could charm the pants off of any woman, that man could."

Then Mama would cry. So there was no way I was going to tell Grandma.

When we got home, I ran ahead of her and looked in the mailbox. There was a Sears catalog, some medical supplies for my father, some flower seed that Mama had ordered, and a letter. Just like Serena said, I thought.

The letter smelled of cheap perfume. It was from some woman in Frankfort, Kentucky. I had a feeling not to give it to her, but she'd already seen it.

She grabbed it from me and tore it open. A small picture fell out of it and floated to the floor. I picked it up and tried to hand it to her, but she was too busy reading. The photograph was of a little blond baby. Underneath, in bold letters was written, "Johnny, age one year."

After she finished reading the letter, her face turned the color of ashes. She crunched it in her hand, and dropped it. Then she snatched the picture from me. She looked at it and without saying a word, turned and went into the house. I followed. I couldn't stand the way she looked. Her body seemed to have shrunk. Her shoulders slumped. In a few seconds she had gone from happiness to pain, her hopes dashed in that crumpled piece of paper.

She never went to Serena's again. She said she didn't want to listen to her pack of lies.

The unexpected company never arrived, nor did the money. Nor did I get the coat in Fuller's Store. Somehow, it didn't matter to me anymore. I just wanted Mama to be happy again.

She put the picture of little Johnny in the family Bible. I wondered if I would ever see him, or if he would be forgotten like the dried flowers.

SUMMER OF THE SPIDER

Kentucky, 1943

I was four years old the summer of the spider. It hung suspended like a trapeze artist on a wire fence next to the Baptist Church. A big black spider covered with yellow splotches. Fine orange fuzz sprouted on its long legs. What made it unique was the white gluey substance that spun from its spinneret in up and down strokes that looked like writing. Reverend Aiken said, "The spider has written War. A message from God that the war will go on."

People from miles around came to see the writing spider. And indeed the war went on, taking my friend Billy Burkhart away.

I never knew my father who was killed in a mine explosion four months before I was born. But Billy became my father, for he treated me like a son. He took me everywhere. When he came in his wagon through the woods, heading into town, he always stopped for me and said, "Hop on board, little buddy. I'm going to the store for supplies. I'll buy you a peppermint stick."

Once when we went into the woods to pick blueberries, he cut a branch from a maple tree and whittled a whistle. When it was finished, he put it to his lips and played "Yankee Doodle."

"Show me how to do that," I begged excitedly. He put my fingers on the proper holes and told me to blow. I made a screeching

61

sound and he laughed. Later he made another hole in one end, threaded a shoelace through it and hung it around his neck.

The day Billy went away to war, we had a celebration. The townspeople escorted him to the train station, cheering and yelling "Make us proud, Billy" and "Get that Hitler" and "You show 'em." They tousled his sandy hair. His father held onto him, hugging him. I couldn't say anything. I was sobbing.

Billy knelt and wrapped me in his arms. "Don't cry, little buddy, I'll be back before you know it." He took his whistle from around his neck and put it around mine. "Take care of this for me," he said, and jumped on the train and was gone. I waved until the train was out of sight.

The town stayed busy with the war effort. Mama rolled bandages at the Rebecca Lodge to be sent to the Red Cross. The conveyers clanged day and night bringing coal off the mountain to be loaded into iron gondolas. It was shipped off to the north to defense plants and shipyards. At night the neighbors gathered around Elisha Vaughn's store to listen to news about the war.

The spider stayed on its web, amid a mass of sucked-dry carcasses of flies and bugs.

Several weeks later, in July, I was playing in the front yard when Mama came to the door.

"Come inside, Ethan. I have to get washed up." After scrubbing me spotless, ⸲ dressed me in my sailor suit.

"Mama," I asked, "is it Sunday?"

"No."

"Then why am I wearing Sunday clothes?"

"We're goin' somewhere special."

"Are we goin' to ride the train?"

"No," she answered, gently combing through my damp tangled hair. "But we're goin' to the train station."

"Why?"

"Because someone special is comin' home. Billy's comin' home."

"Billy's comin' home!" I yelled. I couldn't contain my happiness and clapped my hands and jumped up and down. Then I ran to my room and opened the special drawer that held my most prized possessions. Marbles, a yo-yo, a dried tadpole. And most important, the whistle that Billy gave me to save for him. I hung it around my neck, and Mama and I headed for the train station.

A crowd of neighbors and friends filled the station platform. Elisha Vaughn sat at their feet, legs dangling over the edge of the platform, whittling wood and spitting tobacco juice. Mrs. Yates held her baby, her flimsy dress clinging to her from the heat. Mrs. Mills, the postmistress, wiped her face and neck with a handkerchief. The crowd was quiet, not like when Billy left.

My shoes hurt and I asked Mama if I could take them off. She said, "No, we have to look respectable."

Mr. Burkhart's wagon came down the road, the horses kicking up a cloud of dust. He pulled alongside the tracks. He wore an old hat, its band stained with sweat, and his usual overalls. He looked smaller, as if the hump on his back was weighing him down. He spoke to no one, only stared straight ahead.

I heard its whistle long before the train rounded the bend. Then I saw it, puffing steam like a great iron fire dragon. It came to a dead stop. No one got off.

I tugged on Mama's arm. "Where's Billy?"

She put her finger to her lip and said, "Shh, don't talk."

Then the door of the boxcar slid open, and there on the floor was a large box draped in a brand-new red, white and blue flag. Two men jumped down from the boxcar to hoist the box on Mr. Burkhart's wagon. He slapped the reins and the wagon began to move away. We followed like a row of ants crawling across the meadow and into the woods that offered relief from the burning sun.

We trudged through the woods. The sun broke through the clouds, and through the trees, and made shadows on the ground, like long golden fingers.

I was playing a game, pretending to be blind, letting Mama lead me. With my eyes closed I heard Mrs. Mills say, "I never saw a prouder man than Mr. Burkhart the day Billy enlisted. They came into the post office and Mr. Burkhart said, 'I'm thankful to God he gave me a straight and tall son to fight for his country.' In spite of that hump on his back he stretched himself up as if he was standing at attention to salute Ol' Glory."

When I opened my eyes I saw Mr. Burkhart's house of mud and moss-covered stones. Beyond, on a slight rise, I saw a big hole with dirt piled up along one side.

"Mama, where's Billy?" I asked. "Is he in the house?"

"Shh," Mama said again. "I'll tell you later."

Mr. Burkhart climbed down from the wagon and stood at one end of the hole. Reverend Aiken moved next to him. The rest of us gathered around in a circle.

Reverend Aiken began to speak. "Greater love hath no man than to give his life for his friends and country. Not long ago we rejoiced at Billy's leaving. Now we mourn his return."

I wondered what it meant to mourn. The word had a sad sound. While I thought about that, Reverend Aiken said things like, "The war has come home to us. The war killed Billy."

After everyone sang "Shall we Gather at the River", Reverend Aiken said, "Now we commit Billy Burkhart's body to the ground, with certain hope of the resurrection." Two of the men slid leather horse straps around the box and began to lower it into the hole.

I could not stop myself from screaming, "No, no, open the box, open the box! I have to see Billy! I have to give him his whistle!"

Mama pulled me away and we started to hurry out of the woods. I looked back to see Mr. Burkhart, more bent than ever, staring into the hole. I kicked and screamed and hit Mama for not telling me that Billy was in the box. I pulled away from her and ran from the woods and into the meadow. I ran down the lane that led to the Baptist Church and the spider.

And there it was. Fatter than ever. An army of crisp bug carcasses dangled in its web. Although I was out of breath I began to blow the whistle as loudly as I could. Agitated, the spider lifted one of its hairy legs as if to swordfight with me. I picked up a stick from the ground and struck at the spider, yelling, "You killed Billy, you killed Billy!" I slashed until the web tore apart and the spider fell to the ground and scurried away. I followed, still trying to hit it, until it ran into some bushes. I fell to the ground and sobbed bitterly.

Then Mama was kneeling beside me, taking me in her arms and whispering, "Shhhh. No more killings, Ethan, no more. Come on, it's time to go home."

A DRY RESTING PLACE

Hattie pulled her chair in front of the open screen door where she could watch the burial across the street in the cemetery. She balanced a large bowl of shrimp on her lap. Her arthritic fingers moved slowly as she peeled off their transparent shells.

Jesse took the cleaned shrimp and put them in a cauldron of boiling water. He was making etouffee and gumbo.

"Um-um-um. Jesse, would you look at that. Them folks got their own White House, just like the President." Hattie was looking at the white-washed crypts glistening in the morning sun. "I'm gonna have me one of them," Hattie continued. "These old bones gonna have a dry resting place."

"There you go," Jesse answered, "always thinkin' about dyin'."

"When you get as old as me, you'll start thinkin' about it, too," she said.

"Ain't never goin' to think about dyin', just livin'!"

"Well, if you don't quit goin' over to Little Egypt to them Cajun women, you might die young and end up in the Pontchartrain as fish bait."

Jesse ran his hands down over his long white apron, already stained with tomato sauce and roux. "What makes you think you can have one of them 'White Houses'? They ain't for black folks like us."

"They're for anybody who can pay," Hattie said defiantly.

"Well, I heard after a few years they throw your bones out and put someone else's in. I don't want some stranger messing with my leftovers." Jesse laughed.

"Um-um-um. Ain't we particular all of a sudden," Hattie answered.

It was time for the luncheon trade at Commander's Palace. Familiar faces for Hattie. She came there to work when she was a young girl.

Commander's Palace is one of the oldest restaurants in New Orleans, and is located in the Garden District. It is in an aging, long wooden building. There is a downstairs and an upstairs. The upstairs dinner rooms are named after colors--blue, gold, red. They are notorious for their curtained, private alcoves, where rich plantation owners entertained their Creole mistresses.

"Come on, Hattie, I need you to stir the roux," Jesse said.

The Maitre d' came in. "Come away from the door, Hattie. And Jesse, you go change your apron. We have a lot of reservations. Hattie, I hope you made enough key lime pie."

Hattie couldn't pull herself away from the door.

No one knew Hattie had gone to the New Orleans Burial Society. She walked in shyly and took a seat in the waiting area, nodding to one of the men who was also waiting. When her turn came, the young woman at the desk looked Hattie up and down. "Have a seat," she said. "And your name is?"

"Hattie Justine."

"What can I do for you?"

"I wants to know how much one of them crypts is. I wants to be put in one when I die."

"Would that be a single or a double?" the woman asked, flipping one side of her hair.

"A single," Hattie answered. "I ain't plannin' on taking nobody with me." She laughed.

The woman was annoyed. "The price for a single is two-thousand dollars," she said. "How do you wish to pay for it?"

"Cash. I been savin' up money for a long time. I wants a *dry* resting place."

"I'll send papers in the mail for you to fill out." The woman was eager to get rid of her. "When we get the papers back, you can come in and see Mr. Peacock who will take care of you."

"Thank you," Hattie said softly.

When Hattie rode the streetcar back home, she passed the cemetery. "You folks gonna have a new neighbor soon." She sighed.

Yes sir, she thought, I'm gonna be right there with you big shots. My poor daddy buried in that watery grave years ago. A pauper's grave. I tol' myself then I was not goin' to end up like that. No sir, no watery grave for me. I'm gonna have a dry resting place.

* * *

Jesse was going to the cock fights. He caught the ferry over to Little Egypt and went straight to the abandoned cigar factory. The smell inside was overpowering, old tobacco mixed with damp sawdust.

Some of the men there glared at Jesse. They had warned him to stay away from their women.

Just then, two men came in from a side door, holding their birds. All of them gathered around in a circle. One man started by throwing his bird at the other bird. The birds began to jump up in the air, slashing each other with their razor sharp spurs. Blood splattered everywhere, hitting Jesse. The smell of hot blood burned his nostrils. Soon, the first fight was over and Jesse lost his bet.

He went to the vending machine and dropped in two quarters for a Coca Cola. He carried it back to the circle of men. The room was airless and warm. Jesse pressed the cold can to his forehead.

The second fight began, and again Jesse lost his bet. He wasn't discouraged, for there were eight more to go. He stayed until the last fight, picking up his winnings from the floor.

It was around midnight when the fights ended. He headed to the boat landing where he could get a ferry across the river back to New Orleans. Just as he arrived, he saw the ferry pulling out. There was nothing for him to do but stretch out on the riverbank and sleep until morning.

He gazed up at the starry sky. Then
he stretched out on his side and looked at
the river. Suddenly he felt a sharp pain in
his back, then another, and another. He was
vaguely aware of the man standing over him
with a knife.

"We told you not to come back here,"
the man said, and kicked him.

Jesse watched the stars go out, one by
one.

Hattie was worried when Jesse didn't
show up at work the next morning. She knew
he had gone over to Little Egypt. She knew
he had wild ways, like drinking, gambling,
womanizing. Hattie had taken him under her
wing, and tried to steer him in the right
direction. She thought of him as her son by
now. He would laugh at Hattie for worrying
about him. Although Jesse had worked at
Commander's Palace for only one year, Hattie
knew quite a bit about him. She knew he left
a wife in Baton Rouge.

The day passed without hearing anything
from Jesse. Then another, and another.

"I know sumpin' happened to that boy,"
Hattie said to the Maitre d'.

"Oh, he's probably on a drunk and holed
up with some woman."

"No," she said. "I know sumpin's
happened to him."

As Hattie had predicted, the news came
around noon on the third day.

"We found his body on the bank of the Pontchartrain. He was stabbed twelve times," the policeman said.

"Po' boy. Po' boy," was all Hattie was able to say. She shook her head back and forth and wiped her eyes on her apron.

The following day, Jesse's wife showed up from Baton Rouge.

Hattie asked her to sit down. She filled a plate with food for her. They talked. Hattie tried to comfort her.

"I told him not to come up here to New Orleans. It's sin city," she said to Hattie.

"Why don't you stay with me 'til you take his body back to Baton Rouge."

"That's just it, I can't take him. I don't even have enough money to bury him."

That night, after Jesse's wife had fallen asleep on the couch, Hattie sat in front of the fire, thinking. She knew that he could end up in a pauper's grave. Just like what had happened to her father.

She went into the bedroom and took the old shoebox from under her bed, opened it and looked at the two thousand dollars she had saved. She thought of all the things she had done without to save that money. Maybe she could give his wife some of it. That might help.

Later, she was lying in bed, unable to sleep. Can't let that po' boy lie in a pauper's grave, she thought. Then she knew what she had to do.

The next morning over chicory c
she handed the shoebox to Jesse's w
"Here, you take this money and bury that po'
boy."

The following week Hattie was doing
both her work and Jesse's. When she stopped
to rest, she pulled her chair away from the
door and didn't look at the burial taking
place across the street.

"How come you're not watchin' the
goin's on?" the Maitre d' asked.

"Ain't studyin' dyin' no more," Hattie
answered. "When you gives me my pay, I's
gonna buy me a new hat and maybe a new dress,
and soon I'm takin' me a trip to Atlanta, and
I means to go there in style."

WINGS OF AN ANGEL

Pleasant View, Ky.
1942

Father Flanagan
Boys Town, Neb.

Dear Father Flanagan,
I read where you were doing good work with boys that are getting into trouble. I have such a boy. He's my dead sister Leanne's boy. We just can't handle him anymore. By "we" I mean me and my husband Roy.

I thought I'd better tell ya we belong to the Baptist Church. You must be Catholic, being called Father and all. I hope it won't make a difference. I'll be waitin' to hear from you.

Yours truly,
Minnie Kates

P. S. His name is Lester.

Lester was lying under the house on an old car seat he found at Roy's Garage. His tiny frame had managed to pull it up the road. He stopped to rest from time to time, his gingham shirt falling off one thin shoulder. Sweat dampened his red hair. He breathed hard, sucking air through the hole where his front teeth were missing. He pulled and shoved until he got the car seat under the floor of the wood frame house. He hid it behind the brick chimney, where Aunt Min couldn't see it.

* * *

Aunt Min hadn't bothered to get herself dressed to go to Loretta's house. She went up the dirt lane, her plump body in a pink snap-up dress, her flip flops making a slapping sound.

"Loretta, I hope you don't mind me barging in on you," she said, letting the door slam behind her.

"Lord, no," Loretta answered. "You know you're always welcome." She went over to the cast iron stove and poured two cups of coffee from a speckled pot. With a cigarette dangling from her lower lip, she carried them over to the table.

"Now, what's bothering you, Min?" she asked.

"Oh, it's Lester."

"What's he done now?"

"Well, he's being accused of stealin' Mrs. Cranks' pin. And now he's got me and Roy fightin'."

"What about?"

"Lester said he saw Roy kissin' that Heltin girl in back of his garage."

"Did you ask Roy about it?"

"Yeah, but he denies it, had a fit, and said Lester was lyin' and if I didn't send him to his daddy in Kansas City, he was going to leave and join the army."

"What did you say?"

"I told him the army would have to be hard up to take an ol' fart like him."

"What did he say then?"

"'You'll see', he said. Told me it's either him or Lester."

"What are you goin' to do, Min?"

"I don't know. I wrote to Father Flanagan, you know I told you about him. I'm waitin' to hear from him."

"Poor little tyke," Loretta said. "I can still see him holding Virgil's hand. Virgil was so drunk he could hardly walk. Lester had to steer him around like a seein' eye dog. It's a wonder he ain't dead, feedin' him them Moon Pies and Coca Colas in Farley's Cafe."

"I know, it was a shame," Min said, shaking her head.

"Why do you think Virgil left him?"

"I don't know. It liked to killed the little fella. You remember he didn't talk for almost six months."

Lester didn't like Mrs. Cranks. Every time he went to the post office, she said, "No letter from that good-for-nothing daddy of yours." She'd grin, showing one gold tooth. "You should be grateful that your Aunt Min is giving you a Christian upbringing."

What if I did take the pin, Lester thought. It belonged to my mother. Aunt Min gave all of her things to the Church bazaar, and Mrs. Cranks got the pin at the auction. She shouldn't have took it.

Lester heard thunder roll through the mountain. It sounded like a truck running over the bridge. But he was secure under the house. He had everything he needed--his father's hunting knife, his mother's picture and handkerchief that smelled of her perfume, and now, her pin. He picked up his Captain Marvel comic book and started to read.

"Take that, you varmit," he yelled, his fist clenched.

He was boxing with the wind.

"Loretta, I just have to tell you the latest." Min reached into her laundry basket and shook out a wet sheet.

Loretta settled herself on a tree trunk.

"Well, Lester told me he was peekin' through the window at the Baptist parsonage and he saw Reverend Higgins and Deacon Smith dancing together. Lester said they were both naked as a jaybird."

Loretta laughed out loud. "What a picture that must've been."

"I told Roy, no way could I look at them without my face turning red.

"And that's not all, Loretta. Roy says we have to go to some church. We can't let Sunday go by without worshipping somewhere, so we went to the Holy Roller Church across the river. We didn't know they were going to handle snakes or I wouldn't have gone."

"Snakes?"

"Yes. And do you know what Lester did?" Min said.

"No, what?"

"He inched his way up to the vestibule where they had them snakes in a burlap bag. Lester opened the bag and peeked in. I was so scared. I tried to get to him, but everybody was shouting in the aisle. Then you know what he did?"

"What?" Loretta asked, becoming breathless.

"Well, he dumped them snakes out on the floor. There were rattlers and copperheads running everywhere."

"Lord, Min, it's a wonder one of them didn't bite Lester."

"Well, I guess they knowed somehow that Lester was meaner than they was."

Lester waited until he knew Aunt Min and Uncle Roy had finished their supper. He snuck into the house and into the kitchen and snatched a piece of chicken from a platter. He took a cigarette from Roy's package of Old Golds and a match from a matchbox. He went out and crawled back under the floor of the house. After he finished the chicken leg, he put a cigarette into his mouth and struck the match. It burned his fingers. He dropped it on the mattress, which quickly caught fire. Lester rolled out from under the porch as the flames started to rise.

Dear Father Flanagan,

Lester's gone and done it now. He's burned us out of house and home. We're forced to live in the back of Roy's garage.

You've got to help us.

Sincerely,
Minnie Kates

Dear Mrs. Kates,

At first, I thought Lester was just a mischievous child. Now I realize it is much more serious. If you'll bring him here, we'll take him in.

Sincerely,
Father Flanagan

Lester had no idea where Nebraska was. Aunt Min had told him she was taking him there.

Lester was sitting in an old green Plymouth that Roy was working on. He turned on the radio and heard Roy Acuff singing, "If I had the wings of an angel..."

I'll bet my mother has wings of an angel, Lester thought. She was good. They say I'm bad, that I tell lies. But I don't. And I don't steal, either. I only took the pin because it was my mother's.

Roy and Min were arguing.

"I promised Leanne, on her deathbed, I'd take care of him."

"Min, you know it's for the boy's good."

"I don't know that. Nebraska's so far away."

Lester took an old yellowed letter from his shirt pocket. It was from his daddy: "Sorry I ran off and left you. It's not because I don't love you, 'cause I do. It's just that you remind me so much of your mother. I had to get away."

* * *

It was a cold November morning. Aunt Min had trouble getting the car started. Finally it kicked in, and she and Lester were on their way to Nebraska.

Lester was very quiet for a while, and then said, "Why do I have to go to that ol' boys school? Why can't I stay with you?"

Aunt Min pulled the car over to the side of the road, and sat there, thinking. What do I have in this town? A husband that cheats on me, and gossipy neighbors, all hypocrites. A minister and a deacon you can't trust...

Then she looked at Lester. "I'm not taking you to Nebraska, to that school. I'm takin' you to your daddy's in Kansas City." She paused. "You know something, I'm staying there, too. There's nothin' for me in this Godforsaken town. Take one last look, Lester. We'll never see it again."

THE TEMPTATION OF REB ISAAC

Reb Isaac was a saintly man. Not only because he went to the synagogue every day to pray, but because he was always ready to help the needy, the sick and the dying. He was a very wise man, and people of the little *shtetl* came to him with their problems. They looked up to him and took his advice. When he went to the well, there was always someone who would say, "I'll carry your water for you, Reb Isaac" or "I'll fix the hole in your roof, Reb Isaac."

It was the holiday season in the *shtetl*. Chanukah for the Jews and Christmas for the Polish Christians. Reb Isaac was weary from the rituals and from sitting by sickbeds. He pulled his long black coat closely to his body. His broad-brimmed black hat was insufficient in the cold wind. He trudged slowly on his way home from the synagogue. Ice formed in his beard. As he passed a Polish house, he heard a baby crying. Without thinking, he raised the leather strap on the gate and went inside.

A baby lay on a blanket spread on the cold floor. Reb Isaac pulled a rocker close, gently took the baby in his arms and began to rock. There was no one around. The house was sparsely furnished and there was very little heat.

Just then a woman rushed in with a small boy. She was very beautiful, with golden braids wrapped around her head. Reb Isaac hastily looked at the floor, for it was forbidden for Hassidic Jews to look at women.

"I know you're wondering why I left my baby alone. We needed wood for the stove, so I went to help Jonah carry some. Everyone was waiting in line to do their holiday baking."

Looking away, Reb Isaac said, "I understand. I'll be on my way now."

As he was leaving the widow's house, two devout Jews saw him.

"Reb Isaac," one said, "how could you go in that house with icons and crosses?"

"I did not see the icons and crosses," he replied. "I heard a baby crying."

He continued on his way. How beautiful she is, he thought. I know I was not supposed to look at her, God, but her radiance was such that I could not lower my eyes. I will not think of her again.

But as the days passed, he thought of her. And of the baby that had no crib. I know, he thought, I'll make a crib for it. Don't tempt God, Isaac. The first time you entered her home, you had a reason--a baby was crying. But if you go back, the Elders of the synagogue will bring you up before them. On the other hand, God, I don't think you'll punish me for making a cradle for a baby. The Gentile Baby Jesus had no cradle. I promise, God, when I take the cradle to her, I won't look at her.

84

Reb Isaac went into the woods and cut down a tree. He sawed off a portion big enough for a cradle. Being very good with his hands, he hollowed it out and planed it until the wood felt smooth as silk. He covered an old pillow in white muslin to make a bed. He took a prayer shawl that had belonged to his wife, Hannah, thinking, I know you won't mind me using it for a baby's head. Forgive me, Hannah, for looking at the widow, but you've been gone so long and I do get lonely. He stained the wood a honey tint and set the crib aside to dry.

I should have something for the boy, he thought. After all, it is their Christmas. He thought and thought. I'll give him the dreidel I found at the synagogue. Boys like spinning tops.

Chanukah was over, but it was now Christmas Eve for the Christians. Isaac gathered the food that neighbors had brought him for Chanukah--chickens and a goose, sweet meats, fruits--and put it all in a sack next to the cradle and dreidel. Looking around the room, he saw the Menorah candles that had not burned all the way down. These will help brighten her house, he thought.

He set off, singing as he walked, "Die-De-Die-Die-Dee." Isaac, it's a sin to be so happy, he told himself.

He knocked on the widow's door, then stared at the ground. The door opened and he found himself looking down at her worn shoes that had no buckles.

"Won't you come in," she said.

"No, no, I can't. I brought you some things for your Christmas."

"What a beautiful cradle," she exclaimed. When she reached to take it from him, she accidently touched his hand.

"Oh, you're trembling," she said. "Come in and I'll give you a glass of tea."

"No, no, I couldn't," he answered, still looking down.

"Let me repay you, please," she said, reaching up to lift his chin so his eyes met hers.

He could not answer for a moment. Oh, God, he thought, are you striking me blind for looking at her? Why should it be a sin to look at her? Why should it be a sin to look at someone so beautiful? Then he said aloud, "I will have the tea."

She pulled a chair away from the table for him to sit on. They talked, and she told him that her husband had been dead only three months and how lonely she was.

He drank the tea hurriedly and told her he had to be on his way.

The next day when Reb Isaac was shopping for the Shabbas, he spied a pair of silver buckles in a store window. Before he had time to think, he went into the store and bought them.

"I'll have to go back one more time, God," he said aloud. "Just to give her the buckles, God. I promise I will not see the widow again."

As he walked to the widow's house, he sang a little song: "Die-Dee-Die-Die-Dee, De-Die-Die."

He knocked softly on the widow's door. There was no answer. He knocked again, this time louder. Still no answer.

Just then a neighbor passed by. "Are you looking for the widow? She's gone."

"Gone? Gone where?"

"She made the quota and left for Southhampton, England. From there she will take a ship to America."

Reb Isaac felt an emptiness in his stomach and an ache in his heart. He walked home. This time he did not sing, but instead talked to God:

"Was it too much to ask? Something beautiful for these old eyes? Someone to sit by the fire with. Someone to share my life?" He took a deep breath. "Isaac, why are you questioning God? He knows best, and he knows it wouldn't have worked out. Forgive me, God, for questioning you. Thank you for removing the temptation."

MADDIE

"Why did Skylar have to go all the way to New Orleans to get a wife? Plenty of single women right here in Kentucky. The women in our little town weren't good enough for him, I guess."

"You mean some of your pale-skinned, thin lipped bible-thumpers? Take a look at them, and then look at Maddie. There's your answer. Why if I was a young man..."

My aunt spotted me and said, "You get out of here, Lenore. This conversation is not for your eight-year-old ears."

My grandfather and Aunt Amanda were arguing about Maddie again. Lately, that was all they talked about.

I couldn't figure out what all the trouble was about. I loved Maddie. She brightened up our big old intimidating house.

"Come on honey, don't be so stiff. Move your shoulders a little more." Maddie showed me how to do it, her shoulders moving rhythmically to the music from our dusty victrolla. I'd never seen anyone dance before. I watched her hips move like a snake. Pulling her billowing skirt up over her knees, she pointed her toes downward. Then with one hand on her hip and the other stretched to heaven, she slithered and swayed, all the time humming to the music in a low moan.

"Maddie, where did you learn to do that?" I asked.

She laughed. "My mother said I was born dancing. She said to me, 'You can dance and you're pretty. You can make your way in the world.' So she turned me out." Her eyes saddened. "I've worked in a lot of jazz joints and gin mills."

I didn't know what a jazz joint or gin mill was.

One day when I was coming home from fishing, I cut across Bessie Calhoun's backyard. There was Mrs. Cates hanging over her fence watching Bessie hang her wash.

"Skylar could've had any woman in this town, instead he had to go off and marry a Creole." Mrs. Calhoun stopped long enough to swat a summer fly buzzing around her head.

"She's been here almost two months and she ain't been to church yet. She wears that big crucifix around her neck, makes them funny signs across her chest. She must be one of them pagans," Mrs. Cates said.

"God only knows what kind of diseases she's brought in on us," Mrs. Calhoun chimed in.

Just then, they saw me and shut up.

It made me angry the way everyone treated Maddie. When we went to the store, the women stopped talking, dropping their eyes to the floor.

"Why do they do it, Maddie?" I asked.

"I reckon some folks are just born mean. Don't you go looking for trouble. Trouble'll find you soon enough."

"Have you seen troubles, Maddie?"

"Lot's of 'em," she answered. "The best luck I ever had was when I met your uncle Skylar. Oh, I know he drinks a lot and gambles, but he's a good man. It was the best day of my life when he asked me to marry him and took me away from my troubles."

"How did you meet him, Maddie?"

"One night in New Orleans he was drinking too much and got sick. I took care of him. After that, every time he came to New Orleans he stayed with me." Her eyes got all misty.

I liked it when Uncle Skylar went off on one of his gambling sprees, it gave me time alone with Maddie. She told me stories about New Orleans.

"Honey, there's a house in New Orleans where this woman lives and she can cast a voodoo spell on people, and make 'em act like a dog or anything. This house is hidden way back behind palm trees and man-eating plants. The second floor has a wrought iron railing. The courtyard is made of red bricks. When this woman gets tired of her boyfriends, she has her houseboy push 'em off the balcony and the man-eating plants dee-stroys the evidence." Maddie threw her head back and laughed.

I didn't know if her stories were true. I only knew I liked being with Maddie.

"Maddie's a bad influence on Lenore," I heard my aunt say to Grandpa. "I don't like her telling her all those strange stories about New Orleans, and teaching her to dance. Dancing is the devil's tool."

91

"Leave her alone," my grandfather said. "She's the only one I've seen her take to since her mother and father died. You just can't stand to see someone having a good time. You should have married a long time ago, Amanda."

"Go on, take her side. But I heard from Mrs. Cates that she heard from a travelin' salesman that Skylar found her in a bordello." She ran her hands over her gray, snatched-back hair.

I wondered what a bordello was. I envisioned a grand hotel, where the women wore fine clothes made of lace, and wore silk stockings and carried silk parasols. Where the men drank something called absinthe, in dark rooms, like Maddie told me.

A year after Maddie came to live with us, Uncle Skylar died. I didn't feel sad or anything. After all, he wasn't around that much anyway.

I heard Grandpa tell Aunt Amanda that, "Skylar left a large gambling debt and it's going to take his inheritance to pay it off."

I became frightened for Maddie. My aunt said, "From now on I make the rules around here and there will be no more dancing. If Maddie isn't careful, there'll be no more Maddie."

I told her what Aunt Amanda said.

She just laughed and said, "Don't you worry your pretty little head none. I'll be alright." She held me in her warm arms. To console me, she let me listen to the ocean in her conch shell. To my surprise, when I lifted it to my ear, a small stone fell from it and rolled on the floor, like it had a life of its own.

"What's this, Maddie?" I asked, turning the stone in my hands.

"That's my wishstone," she replied.

"What's a wishstone?"

"Well, some folks have a wish book and some folks have a wish bone, but I have a wish stone." She laughed.

"What's it for, Maddie?"

"When I want something real bad, I rub the stone and make a wish."

"Does it come true?"

"Every time."

"Can I make a wish, Maddie?"

"No, honey. Only the one that owns the stone can do that. Then you have to be very careful what you wish for or you may get stuck with something you don't want." Maddie put the stone back inside the conch shell.

She was doing more and more of the work around the house. Grandfather had taken to his bed since Skylar's death. She took care of him as well as all the cooking. Aunt Amanda said, "She might as well earn her keep."

The house seemed to come alive with the smell of spices that Maddie had brought from New Orleans. She made something called gumbo and jambalaya. It was very hot. My aunt grabbed for the water, saying, "I think she's trying to kill us."

One day Aunt Amanda asked Maddie to cut and fix her hair like the New Orleans women wore theirs. When Maddie was finished, I could see that Aunt Amanda was very pleased with herself. She looked in the mirror and puckered up her face, closing one eye and smiling.

Once when Mrs. Cates and Bessie Calhoun came to visit, Aunt Amanda asked Maddie to fix their hair. I watched her as she clipped away, the hair falling to the floor. Some of it, she put in the pocket of her apron.

Another time, I caught Maddie cutting a small piece of material from the hem of one of Aunt Amanda's favorite dresses.

"Why are you doing that?" I asked.

"I'm just trying to keep mean folks in line," she answered.

I didn't think anymore about it.

Another time, Maddie asked me to bring her scissors from the dresser drawer in her bedroom. I was puzzled, because there in the drawer were three small rag dolls with real hair. It was the hair I saw Maddie put in her pocket. I thought they were pin cushions, because they had pins sticking in them.

The next day, Aunt Amanda came running down the hall with her dress that had the piece of material taken from it.

"Who did this?" she yelled.

"I did it," I answered. I couldn't let Maddie take the blame. It was just the excuse my aunt needed to send her away.

"Why did you do it?" my aunt screamed, all the time shaking me.

"Lenore didn't do it. I did," Maddie said, drawing herself up. She seemed to grow before my very eyes.

Aunt Amanda stood stunned. Her face turned a bruised shade of red. "I want you to go, Maddie. I want you to leave as soon as possible."

The next day was Sunday. In church, I noticed the attendance had dwindled considerably. Especially the women folks. Mrs. Cates was there, but there was something wrong with her throat. She couldn't say a word and she couldn't sing a note. I watched as Mrs. Calhoun twisted and squirmed in her seat. She had a rash all over her body and it was keeping her busy scratching.

Instead of Aunt Amanda shaking hands with the preacher as she always did, she grabbed him and danced him up the aisle, singing loudly, "There'll be a hot time in the old town tonight."

The congregation went crazy. Some of them started to shout. The men stood with their mouths hanging open.

Mrs. Cates yelled, "Amanda, you're going to hell."

The next day I went to the train station with Maddie. She held me close and I began to cry.

"Oh, Maddie, I'll never see you again."

"Hush, honey," she said. "You'll see me. When you get older, you'll find me." She took both my hands and pressed something into them and closed my fingers tightly around it. "This is yours now. Remember to use it wisely, only for things you really want. Maybe to be a famous writer, like you told me. Promise me you'll only use it for good things." She kissed me and got on the train.

I opened my fingers and there was the glowing stone that had fallen from the conch shell. Wiping my tears, I yelled after her, "I promise...I promise."

I heard her laughter long after the train had gone.

JEWEL OF THE NILE

"Here she comes, boys," Andy said, placing his clippers on the counter by the barber's chair, and turning Joe Cutchen around so he could see outside.

"Yeah, twelve o'clock noon exactly," Joe Cutchen said.

You could set your watch by Ruby's arrival at the Pleasant View barbershop, where she stopped to look at the barber pole, following its movement with her body.

She rolled her head in a snake-like fashion, following the colors curling upward. Then she began to twist her body to mimic the barber pole.

"She sure can dance," Isome Jones said. "Always could, even before the accident. I never saw anyone move like she can."

Isome had a crush on Ruby since their grade school days. He sat behind her in class and used to tug gently on her long red pigtails. She didn't seem to mind.

One day, back then, he was out walking and heard that there had been an accident on the railroad tracks. He was the first one to reach the car where it sat smashed.

Ruby and her parents were inside the car. They'd been on a Sunday outing when they got stuck on the tracks and a train hit them full force, severing Ruby's parents' heads. She survived without a scratch, but was permanently traumatized. When Isome got to her, she didn't recognize him. She sat looking at the crossing lights flickering back and forth.

Several days had passed and Ruby had not been to the barbershop.

"I tell you, boys, somethin's happened to her. She wouldn't stay away like this," Isome said.

Joe Cutchen laughed and said, "Next, you'll want to marry her."

"When she comes back, I'm gonna ask her to marry me. I'll take care of her."

Ruby was spending all her time at the new carnival in town. She watched the lights on the carousel and Ferris wheel.

Joe Goody had been watching her. He was in charge of the Ferris wheel. "You wanna ride?" he asked.

Ruby shook her head, "No."

"Like to watch the lights, huh, kid?"

Ruby shook her head, "Yes."

"Too bad we're leaving town after closing tonight."

At that, Ruby began to cry.

"Hey c'mon, kid, if you like the carnival that much, why don't you come with me? We're only moving to the next county."

Ruby shook her head, "Yes."

"Go home and get your things and meet me back here at midnight, kid." He pointed to 12:00 on his watch.

"You better be careful," Carl, one of the barkers, said. "She looks like jailbait to me."

"She's old enough," Goody said, winking. "I'll send her home after a night or two."

"After all the women you've had." Carl shook his head. "On top of it, she's fat."

"Okay by me, I like 'em fat. Did you ever see how their hips move up and down, like the haunches on a horse?"

Isome went to the police station. He asked Sergeant Fraley if he knew about Ruby being missing.

"You're the twentieth person who's asked me that. Seems the whole town is worried about her."

I'm gonna ask her to marry me, Isome thought. I'll take care of her.

The carnival trailers were lined up in a row, ready to go. Ruby was asleep on the couch.

Sure looks tempting, Joe Goody thought. But there'll be time for that later.

After Goody had finished helping set up the carnival rides, he went back to his trailer. As he got closer, he heard music coming from inside. His radio. Through the window, he saw Ruby dancing to the music. Her body moved like a well-oiled machine. One hip undulating upward, then the other. Up and down. She shimmied and shook, the rolls of fat crawled up her mid-section. She was very graceful. Her face looked completely innocent, as if she didn't know what her body was doing.

"Well, what have we here?" Goody said out loud. "This kid can sure dance. I might be able to make some money with her."

He went right over to the Dancing Dolls tent, looking for the manager.

"Hey, Bob," Goody said, "I got a kid that can really dance."

"Oh?"

"You've never seen the likes of her."

"Well, you're in luck today," the manager said. "Just so happens one of my girls called in sick. So, have her here at seven sharp."

Joe couldn't find Ruby. He ran around looking for her. He went into the food tent.

"Have you seen Ruby?" he asked Carl, who was sipping a cup of coffee.

"Yeah, saw her about an hour ago going into the Fun House."

When Joe found Ruby, she was standing in front of a Mechanical Fat Woman that laughed as she bent from the waist and raised her arms over her head. She did this over and over.

"C'mon, Ruby," Joe said, pulling her arm and dragging her outside. "I got you a job. All you have to do is dance."

Ruby heard the emcee over the loudspeaker.

"This is what you've been waitin' for. The girl with the educated body, if you *know* what I mean. She was the favorite of King Farouk and Sheik Abdullah. Men have been known to faint watching her dance, and we've got her. The Eighth Wonder of the World-- Ruby, Jewel of the Nile."

The men began to clap and yell and stomp their feet.

Ruby paid no attention to any of this. She was too busy looking at herself in the mirror. She looked at how the light played on her costume. Purple panels of gauze hung from a G-string covered in gold sequins. Green spangles hung from her skimpy brassiere.

"You can see the little lady needs some encouragement," the emcee said.

The men yelled even louder this time. "We want Ruby. We want Ruby."

Finally, the manager went into the dressing room and pulled Ruby out on the stage. Ruby stood there, not moving.

"C'mon, honey, let's see what you've got," one man cried.

"Dance, damn you," the manager yelled.

Still, Ruby did not move.

"Hey, what is this?" one man shouted. "Some kind of ripoff?"

"Yeah," chimed in another. "I want my money back!"

Ruby did start to move, but just like the Mechanical Fat Woman in the Fun House, laughing and laughing.

The men got angry. They thought she was laughing at them. "Hey, let's tear this joint apart," one of them said. They began to break up the chairs.

Ruby ran to the dressing room, and out the back door to the trailer. Joe came running in after her.

"You bitch, you get out of here, and don't come back," he shouted. He tossed her suitcase out the door and threw her raincoat at her.

Ruby ran all the way to the main road. It began to rain, drenching her. She was cold now, and she started to cry.

Just then a bus came along. The driver saw her, and at the last minute stepped on the brakes.

He opened the door. "Hey, what are you doing out here in the rain? Where're you trying to go?" he asked.

Ruby didn't answer. She stood there, shivering in her raincoat.

"C'mon, kid, I'll take you to the next town," the driver said. "There's a police station there."

At the police station, Ruby wouldn't answer questions. She stared at the policeman bending over her.

"I'm not going to hurt you," he said. "Where do you live, kid?"

Ruby replied softly, "Pleasant View."

"Pleasant View? Hey, we have something on a missing girl from Pleasant View." He thumbed through the pages of a Missing Persons file. "Yeah, here we are. And you seem to fit the description. I'll drive you over there in the morning. You can sleep in the lockup tonight."

Ruby returned to Pleasant View at 11:45 in the morning. She walked very fast to get to the barbershop at exactly 12:00 noon.

"We missed you, Ruby," Andy said.

"Glad you're back," Mr. Cutchen said. "You gave us quite a scare. Don't ever go away again."

"Ruby, marry me," Isome shouted, running outside and taking her suitcase. "Let me take care of you."

Ruby looked at the barber pole and smiled. She let her raincoat fall to the ground, and in her spangles and sequins began to dance.

DEE GREENBERG - About The Author

DEE is a retired attorney whose interest in the problems of older adults led to her first novel. Born and raised in Chicago, she lives there with her husband of forty-seven years.

SUNFLOWERS

"Why can't you write during the day?" my husband snaps at me. "Work during the day like other people?"

"It's not like that, Jeff. Sometimes, you think about it day and night. You don't just turn it on at nine, and off at five."

"But you start so late. With the typing. Can't you roll into it before eleven? or noon?"

I sense bigger criticism coming. I know that voice. His probing, lawyer voice is taking over.

I watch him lean forward and put an elbow on the glass-topped breakfast table. I look at his suntanned face--so smooth, young-looking. He could be a guy who dishes up ice cream, or caddies on a golf course as an after-school job instead of a man who's been practicing law for over twenty years.

"Paula, you're at the computer all night," he says.

"Oh, really." I grip my cigarette, almost break it in half. "Well, you're not home half the nights, anyway."

As usual, when this happens I get scared. It could turn into one of those things we do lately where I hold back tears and get short of breath. The immediate impact of starting another big scene. Suddenly I feel we are entombed here, sealed in behind the sliding doors of this blue and yellow breakfast room. A room we could've only dreamed about back in the seventies when we were newlyweds.

He starts to fill his wallet with credit cards. I light a fresh cigarette. In an hour he'll be off to the Bar Association convention downtown and I'll wait for the landscapers, who will manicure the lawn and shrubs of this four-bedroom piece of perfection that occupies one of the best corner lots in Skokie, Illinois.

He gets up now. "So, are you coming down later?" he asks, standing at the white countertop. "There's a reception. And you know I got two tickets for the dinner tonight."

"I can't."

"I want you to show up--"

"No."

He slams his hand against the counter. A faraway part of me starts to shake.

"Okay, okay," he says very quietly, "go for a run. Go visit someone. Do what you want."

I get up, too, slide the door open, then turn around and face him. But, instead of just the mild anger I'm expecting to see in his brown eyes, I see weariness, too.

I should go to you now, Jeff, touch you, say I'll miss you tonight. I should say I'll go with you, meet you. But I can't. Something is gone. I don't even understand what's gone, can't remember anymore. And I can't even tell you I'll miss you tomorrow night, when I stay in town with Liz. My best friend Liz. First night I've been away without you in five years.

A long ash is hanging from my cigarette. We both see it, and he gives me a look. I reach for the ashtray. The ash drops, hits the rim of my coffee mug, spreads out onto the floor.

"Jesus!" He points to the floor, the cherry cabinets, the blue-tiled backsplash over the sink. "The smell. I hate it. You're ruining everything."

You see, once, I could've touched you, and told you I loved you, gone downtown tonight and to a girlfriend's tomorrow. Once, I wore so many hats, was so many women.

"...don't even say hello to me when I come in the door. You know that, Paula?"

But I used to run to the kitchen window when I heard your car in the driveway.

"Paula? You know that?"

"I'm sorry."

A wash of August heat drifts in through the screen. I feel wasted. Any further explanations I should give him are steamed out of me now.

"Paula?"

"Go to hell."

So softly I say this to him. For the first time.

Then, "I'm sorry," comes out of me again.

"Shit," he says, and walks past me, out to the deck.

He's gone now. The sliding door is still open and the sweet smell of cut grass wafts into the room. The landscapers--dark-

haired, muscled men in dampened T-shirts--
are finishing the lawn. I go outside. Lady
of the house surveying the work.

The leader, a man whose muscles don't
fit into the black top he's wearing, smiles
at me as he guides the three-foot-wide mower
around the corner of the house. When he
disappears to the big-street side of our lot-
-where there are no low windows, and tall
hedges protect us from the traffic whizzing
by--I go check my garden. My little path of
beauty that rims one side of the house.

I can almost see things growing when
I'm out here, especially my petunias that
must have a drink of water every day it
seems. The tulips are a memory, of course.
Last May their bulbs sprouted up into cups
of bright yellows, pinks, even a few purples.
But they had a short life.

The odd people here are my sunflowers-
-crazy-looking, always turning, stretching
their fat faces every which way. People tell
me--kid me actually--that sunflowers don't
fit, look strange. But I love them. They
comfort me.

I wander back to the front, stare at
the landscapers' paint-chipped black pickup.
How does it feel when they ride home in it?
I'd like to ride in it, in the back, feel the
wind blowing through my hair. I have an urge
to climb in.

But I only follow the sounds of the
mower, and see they've finished the bushes--
those green, velvety, solid things that river

the hard lines of our tri-level house like a good outfit camouflages a bad figure.

It's about six. After running four times around the park a block away, I keep going, up and down residential streets. I wonder how I must look to people. Are they glancing up from their dinner plates, saying: "She's lost weight. Why did she highlight that long brown hair? Should've just cut it and covered the gray. She's gotta be in her mid-forties."

When I finally head home I think about Liz' high-rise apartment, how it overlooks Lake Michigan and Monroe Street harbor. Buckingham fountain, a few blocks away, shooting colored water toward the night sky. Grant park separating us from the downtown lights. I wish I was going tonight.

At eleven, Jeff isn't home yet. I'm showered and propped up in bed watching a rerun of a cooking show from earlier in the week.

Should've gone with him. Should've gone down and stayed in the studio apartment we have downtown. Our investment apartment. A white-carpeted room with lots of mirrors, shiny new galley kitchen, and a bathroom with Italian tiles. We could've skipped the dinner, the speeches. We could be fused, tongue-deep in each other now. He'd like that.

Then I remind myself of the last time we went there, six weeks ago, after a symphony

concert. After a few drinks at a nearby bar,
too.

I brought along new linens. Had a
silky, above-the-knee, dark green nightie
already in the closet. But the apartment
door wasn't closed two minutes before he
landed two wet kisses on my face. I braced,
tightened inside, as his slack mouth slid
into my lips.

"Put your legs up," he said, after
steering me toward the desk.

We stood there, the skyline of downtown
Chicago on one side and too many mirrors on
the other.

"C'mon, hon," he said. "Come *on*."

A tug, a push, and my legs were up as we
fell onto the couch instead of the desk. With
a shoe off one foot and my panties hanging
around the ankle of the other, I just let him
do it. I pretended and faked it, because I
was sure that if I didn't do it fast he was
going to throw up all over us.

Dozing and waking, I think about the
apartment.

Finally, I hear our car in the
driveway.

But when Jeff comes upstairs, I turn
toward the window, keep my eyes closed.
Soon, all the lights go out and he eases into
bed. I stay facing away from him. After
he's asleep, I turn over, see the curve of
his shoulder under the sheet, and I want to
press against him. And I don't want to.

Later, a terrible dream: Jeff is
standing over me. Then he is pulling up my

dress while men in white coats surround us, watching. Many men. I see long, dark steel instruments flash in the half-light.

Then they are inserting these things into me, expertly curving them up into my belly, and I know they're too big but they keep pushing them in and pulling them out, making sucking sounds with each pull. I am screaming, from pain, and from a sudden orgasm. It hurts, but I wait for the next one, the next push. The men are all smiling, and then laughing out loud.

In the morning, the vague feel of instruments--penises, maybe--are still with me. Standing in the kitchen, halving oranges for the juicer, I think about my writing. A few scribbles on paper this week; no new words on the computer. I can't make myself go over to the desk and open the laptop.

I want to cry.

Jeff comes downstairs at ten, two small bags in tow. One has his personal stuff in it, I can tell. "Easier to stay down," he says. After the breakfast meeting that ends the convention, he should "discuss a case" with one of his colleagues. He's got a meeting with a client at eight-thirty in the morning tomorrow. After all, they go to court on Wednesday.

Why this apology? He knows I'm going to Liz' tonight.

At eleven, I feel queasy.

Mom is sitting across from me at the breakfast table, in Jeff's place. I've toasted us each a bagel, spread them with cream cheese, thinking about how Liz and I will run together tomorrow morning before I come back home.

Now Mom is nagging me about how I live these days. She does it with concern, though. But today I can't deal with it. I feel mild panic, then a sense of failure, like I did after the miscarriage. "You'll get pregnant again," they told me. "You'll try again." I tried. I didn't get pregnant again. Soon, I didn't care, started to spend too much money.

Tomorrow I'll tell Liz about the mess I'm in. Carefully. Can't spill it all. And tomorrow, we'll fly past the harbor, past the band shell--set apart from the crowds pushing into the Loop a few blocks away. We'll sweat. And we'll talk...

Mom is watching me.

"Paula, what do you want, someone to sit down and write stories with you?" She leans forward. "He gives you everything."

I stare at this woman. At her exercised, sixty-two-year-old body, her blond eyebrows and smooth face. Her almost-taut, tanned upper arms. Independent lady who runs a business with her sister, and is pissed because I don't want to work there anymore. She vacations at resorts where Daddy spends most of his time playing golf. Happy with herself. A big strong bird, she is.

"*Oy,*" she says, and looking pained when I don't answer, repeats, "*Oy.*"

"Ma!"

"He loves you," she says. "Not like your cousin Sherwin, the *meshuggana.* Left Natalie with a baby. Aah, he was always a little sex-crazy. She should've nipped in the bud. Nipped it in the bud--"

"Ma! Ma, what are you talking about?"

She reaches into the bowl of fruit between us, pulls out an orange, starts to peel it.

"Honey? Paula, honey, remember how Daddy was always working, too?"

"It's not that...exactly."

"You have it good. Jeffery loves you. Let him work, don't bother him so much." She reaches forward, tugs at my sleeve. "Estelle. You remember Estelle?"

"Yeah. So? So her husband went out alone every two weeks. That was over thirty years ago. I'm not saying he can't go out."

But I remember eavesdropping on Estelle and Mom one morning as they sat at our Formica kitchen table.

"Stag parties," Estelle said. "Comes home and wants it different this time." And more words--fixed in my mind. "Comes home all hot and excited. You have to get it ready for them, yet. All they want is a good lay." A good lay...

Mom and I finish our breakfast in relative silence.

Later, out in the driveway, I hug her, kiss her on the cheek. But before we move apart, she whispers, "You should've had a baby. You should've adopted."

Mid-afternoon. I'm showered and dressed in a pair of white shorts and an aqua T-Shirt. What'll I tell Liz tonight? We'll loll in a cafe along the Chicago River, have a burger and a beer. So how should I start? With the insular freedom of the city, no one watching, what will I say? Funny how I used to have that same sense of freedom and relief when we moved to the suburbs years ago.

Before I start to pack, I pick up the phone, dial Jeff's number. Don't know why. His voice mail answers. I hang up.

That's not all he wants, is it? A good lay? Do I care anymore?

The day will come when I know what I want, though. Has to. But not here, I'm thinking. Not in this place, where I am stopped of thinking. Everything so stopped.

I go into the bedroom, start picking up credit cards, grabbing my pill bottles and a magnifying mirror. All go into a tote bag. I empty a drawer of shorts and tops, take a ton of undies--stacking it all into a large, double shopping bag.

I sit in the car, still in the driveway. Bags in the back seat. Disks of stories I've done, hard copies of the five short stories I've written this year, and notebooks, journals--all lying on the passenger seat. Twenty minutes pass. Then the house draws me back inside.

I drag a navy nylon suitcase off the closet shelf in the bedroom. My heart pounds like hammers on a kettle drum. Dresses, shoes, whatever it will take to pack the bag tight. Then the unpublished novel, which has been my identity and my sadness for three long years, it goes into another shopping bag. And I'm thinking of twenty years with him and I'm thinking of nothing--at the same time.

Outside again, I dial Liz on the cell phone.

"Paula? Something wrong?"

"Can I stay? For a few days?" My voice is light, shaky. "I'll cuddle the cat, give him TLC. Look after things while you're at work." I take a breath that's followed by sudden tears. "You--you don't have to take sides. It won't be like that."

"What is it, honey?"

"You don't have to take sides."

"Paula, just come on in."

The passenger seat, the back seat--all piled high with my stuff.

I back out of the driveway and park at the curb, motor running. I look at our shaded windows. At the carved bushes. The lawn. I can feel a tiny part of me breaking off and it's so like the shaking I felt yesterday morning. And it hurts. Hurts so much. I sit there. Lady in a deep-orchid,

Chevy sports car, suddenly thinking about running the car onto the lawn, against the bushes.

But I only slide open the sunroof, and finally pull away. Finally. A breeze swirls in, ruffles my bangs.

I think of my flowers. They might panic, might die.

Not the sunflowers, though. They'll hold up a long time. Unlike me, they fight for life very calmly, confidently, because they are completely themselves wherever they live.

At the intersection two blocks away, I picture our street. It's like a frantic board game. People moving and jumping and landing, and, winning or losing, always playing again--never really leaving the square. Never leaving the board.

NEVER

A watch with the insides showing. Naked in front of him.

Even so, one dark snowy afternoon, hidden in our blue-and-gray refuge from the rest of the ward, using our time slot in the tiny room like a prostitute and her customer would, I feel an unexpected sense of closeness to him. Drawn to this thin blond-faced doctor. This man who controls how much longer I have to be a psychiatric patient here.

"Dr. Ryan," I say to him, "when I was married, Steve and I ran around a lot, and I could work, take care of our house--everything."

"Things change," he says.

"Right. Can't be fired up all the time. Not now, at middle age. Right?"

"Probably not."

Of course, he guesses already what my married life was like. What the sex was like. How little I wanted it. Every time we did it, love was, at best, a very thinly disguised mutual masturbation. Maybe not in the beginning, though. But toward the end, when Steve would come home at night--or come near me at all, even if it wasn't for sex--I'd cringe. Cringe, then shake inside.

Dr. Ryan waits.

"Well...after the divorce, when I moved to the same building with Mom? Bad as being married again. God! No matter what I was trying to tell her, she'd give me this,

`Okay, okay', which really meant I shouldn't bother her. But, boy, if she wanted to show me off to her friends--"

"This is my daughter," he says suddenly, grinning, doing a pretty good imitation of a woman he's never known.

"Yes. My daughter, the puppet." I laugh. "See her run. Didn't I do a good job with her? No, wait--on her!"

He laughs too, nodding up and down.

"Eight years. For eight years we were together in that building, and she didn't give a damn what I thought. But I know what a lousy mother she was."

He nods again, as if he knows it, too.

"How her eyes would shine when Janet came over." I wait for the familiar pain to trickle into my chest. It does. "See, I'm the baby. She's two years older than me, but Mom thought she knew everything. And when Janet--from the time Janet passed the bar exam, we had to hear about all her troubles."

Ryan folds his hands in his lap. "She listened to her."

"Even if it was nonsense. `Let's ask your sister Janet', and `Janet says.' Sickening. And I just--just stood it. And my sister didn't do much to stop it, either."

His face is very serious now.

"Wasn't like she wanted me to do heavy work. Oh, no. She just wanted someone to agree with her, always do things her way.

"So many times I'd hang up on her-- when I was calling to see if she was okay.

And when I was married? She'd start
me on the phone! Shouldn't streak my l _.
Gotta gain weight, stay out of the sun. I
wasn't `strong', like Janet. Well, it would
build and build, and I'd just have to decide
whether it would be after the next sentence,
or the next, and bang, I'd slam that receiver
down..."

Those last few weeks with her push back
into my mind. The hospital, intensive care.
The sea of tubes, wires, monitors that became
a part of her decaying body.

"You just couldn't reason with her.
Couldn't. But before she died, when she was
in the hospital, we finally had a few normal
moments."

He tilts his chin upward. "Because?"

"Because...we were more...equal. And
she had to listen. Depend on me, too. I
mean, I was in charge all year, but last
summer she didn't have a choice. She had to
listen to me. Not Janet. Not Steve. Me!"

Ryan sets his thin lips in a tight
line. I dig my fingers under my thigh, press
them against the coarse blue fabric of the
chairseat. A look of mild expectancy washes
onto his expression and my chest starts to
pound.

"She used to call him," I say.

He narrows his eyes at me.

"She kept calling. Yes. Even after the
divorce. Can you imagine?" I take a breath.
"But, last summer... See, last summer, I was
running things."

"It felt good."

"It felt wonderful."

Mid-afternoon. Sitting in the dayroom. Boxes of games strewn out on one of the long tables, a tray of half-eaten lunch on another. Everyone seems to be away. Maybe watching television, visiting with family, talking to therapists.

Still thinking about last summer.

I'd been going to school, part-time. Signed up for only one summer class, though. I met a man there I couldn't take my eyes off of.

By August I found all kinds of reasons to study with him. We started having lunches together. Then dinners. He was very attentive. At first it was a shy, hesitant relationship, with only emotional closeness. Then the magnetism took over.

Finally I got the nerve up to say yes to a night out of town. So uncharacteristic of me, that maybe we should stay somewhere overnight. But we were on the phone. It was easier.

It went on for four dizzying months. Through Mom's death, through Janet's not-so-gentle interrogations about why I couldn't tell her who he was. It went on in town, out of town, but not in the apartment he'd shared with his wife. When he'd talk about her, hint at why they weren't getting along, I'd listen politely. I tried to be understanding, but always thought, "Don't make this a mental threesome." It was tempting to talk about

Steve, though. I resisted, did it only once.

Sometimes, in the apartment where Mom no longer was, a gut-wrenching sadness would come over me. Paralyzing. Many mornings I wouldn't want to go up there at all.

But the thought of seeing him would un-paralyze me. His tall, lean body. The shock of thick brown hair that would fall over his brow at times. His deep brown eyes. The almost absence of lines or wrinkles. So unlike me, with my blond-gray curls, green eyes. So much younger-looking than me-- unless you saw us at a distance.

Bottom line was, when he'd say my name, he seemed to be calling a different girl out to play. One who'd been hiding, who'd never lived like that before.

Two days later, after giving me the go-ahead smile, Ryan looks down, and gently, but quickly, smooths one of the pleats in his beige twill slacks. Then he fixes his eyes in my direction, and waits.

I decide to start with the divorce stuff.

"It wasn't like we had kids. It was a clean break. So why did she still ask him for legal advice?"

But suddenly my mind is racing to think of a pose, an action that will show him how normal I'm getting. Show him I'm getting better. But I feel odd--like a small animal about to be attacked, and trying to look normal only makes it worse. I watch how he folds his hands in his lap now. Body so casual. Too casual.

Haven't told him about the affair yet. So far, kept that from him. Yet, a little tremor starts in me thinking about it. Four months of being in the limbo-land of an affair with a married man. Younger, married man. And God, those bitter, goodbye words. Cold words--mostly from me. Cold as the air outside that December day...

Of course Ryan's been probing, gently, into all that happened just before I ended up here. I'm very guarded about it, say it was "everything." A bad day, a bad week, I tell him. Straw-that-broke-the-camel's-back theory and all that. Just don't know what the straw was, I tell him.

So I babble. He listens, makes occasional interventions.

"Janet was going on a ski trip," I say. "I was house-sitting. You know, plants and stuff. Feed the cat. I thought I'd go downtown, enjoy the Christmas glitter. Meet someone for lunch."

"Sounds nice."

"She did ask if I'd be okay. I said I'd be fine. Finals were over. I'd relax."

"The pressure was off," he says.

Now I want to tell him what else she said.

She was packing. I was sitting on the edge of her bed looking at the array of socks, thermal underwear, ski masks. All about to go into her suitcase. In the middle of reciting what a great place Snowmass was, and how she really needed this trip, she turned to me with an almost loving expression on her face. "I hope he isn't married," was all she said. I didn't answer.

Now I feel totally wasted, start babbling about little things. Nonsense things. Don't even know what. He listens, makes the usual appropriate interventions. He can be so polite sometimes no matter what garbage or gibberish I say.

But his eyes dart to the clock, the face of which I can't see. The hated clock--telling him how much time we used up.

"Men," I say.

"Men?"

I don't answer.

To his left, outside the filmy hospital window, a wash of light-yellow sunshine is falling from the January sky.

End of the week. I'm edgy, more confused than last week. Even with all the drugs they're stuffing into me. Maybe that's it. Drugs.

Another meeting with Ryan. Don't like being with him today.

"So why do you just sit there, draped in the chair like that?" I ask.

He doesn't seem offended, just lifts one pale eyebrow. "I'm listening."

Long pause. I think about the affair. I look at Ryan.

No. Oh, no. No kicks here. Won't tell you anything. Won't tell you how I would press against his warm skin and my own skin would get warm. Hot. Or how we pushed, melted into each other. How we thought we were different. Very different, just because it was us. No. And I won't tell you how I loved to pull him into me, loved to start. How I *still* want to. Never.

But soon, maybe next time, I'll test you. I'll watch your round, featureless face blush when I tell you which body parts are getting old, and sagging, and how I feel desperate about that. It should keep you busy.

I gaze at him. "I can't forget how Janet treated me when Mom was dying. It was bad." I make my voice bitter, full of self-pity. "I was always the one who really took care of her."

He leans forward ever so slightly, his eyes question me for more.

BEACHWALK

It all started last year when my daughter Elaine got pregnant. I found myself taking strange routes home from my job downtown, stopping in the city, sometimes twenty miles from where I live in the suburbs. Talking to strangers. And it's been about a month since I started coming here, to this street--this neighborhood where I grew up.

Today I'm sitting at the end of a not-so-new, faded green bench. At the other end sits a woman in a greasy, blue parka. I stare at her. At her weathered face, her beet-red cheeks. I could tell her what I know about this area. That there used to be an elegant hotel here, right where we're sitting.

Now she is returning my stare, with deadpan eyes.

"There used to be a hotel here," I say to her. Like she was someone I met on the bus, or in a restaurant. I'm acting crazy, I know. "And in back of it, just about where this bench is, there were dazzling white sidewalks. The most beautiful people in the world strolled by."

She puts a grimy, sunburned hand on the edge of the grocery cart at her side. A cart piled high with old magazines, seat cushions, and tightly wrapped plastic bags.

The hotel? The Edgewater Beach Hotel. Long gone, of course. Does she know it was demolished over three decades ago? That its front faced Sheridan Road on the west?

127

But new buildings have taken its place, surrounded its place. Glass and steel and brick. Condos, mostly, except for a retirement community, a supermarket. And Sheridan is bursting with cars these days, too. Cars that want to get out of the neighborhood, cars that want to get into driveways blocked by yet more cars.

This is where I would come when I wanted to dream. How well I remember that. My security blanket.

Now I'm telling her, "Chicago was so beautiful then."

At first, she gives me what I think is a half-smile, keeps staring at me. "Ooh, yes," she says. Then I back off, stop looking directly at her. I've never done this before. I stop talking.

So, we sit with the trees around us. We face the vast expanse of grassy landfill, the distant parade of cars on the Outer Drive--both separating us from the shore of Lake Michigan.

Those dreams were about my future. Had daydreams, too. Back then, I'd stay outside, or go into the lobby, or sit in the passageway that linked the two buildings. I'd sit in a big chair that had ornately-carved legs, and watch ladies whose hair was swept up and held by jeweled combs. Ladies in hip-clinging, silky dresses, strolling arm-in-arm with crisply dressed gentlemen. Sometimes, if I was close enough, I might overhear, "Will this war ever end?"

And when the war did end, and the next one started, I still went there to dream. Even when the old homes in the neighborhood were going down, and I was already a teenager, I went there.

I turn my head to the left, look north along the wall of high-rises, imagining the curve at the end of the Outer Drive a few blocks away. Last stop for express driving. Although the Drive is a parkway, with plantings down the middle--trucks not usually allowed--many of the cars, and the mentality of their drivers, seem to be in a speed mode. There is gridlock in places. Tailgate city.

The drivers will be irritated because they must go local now, take Sheridan if they want to continue north to the city limits, or to the North Shore suburbs. Some will run red lights when they feel like it.

I used to be irritated, too, ran a few "close" reds years ago when I'd zip through here to my new suburban home.

I came here yesterday, too. Left work early--on a Tuesday yet. Wanted to sit, think, and look around. Parked at the Dominick's lot at Foster, and went in to buy groceries, even though I could've waited until I got to home ground to shop.

The lady is repacking her stuff into the cart now. I keep my head down, waiting, waiting for her to go. Go already. I want to be alone. I'm trying to think of something but I don't know what it is. Like when you have to do something important but can't remember what it is, and, for a second it almost surfaces, then goes away.

The place in back of the hotel was the Boardwalk. I know that. But Mom and Daddy called it by another name, too. Beachwalk, I think...

Finally, I see the lady stand up. She dips her head down to look in the cart. Her curved spine bulges through her parka as she bends forward and starts to guide her worldly possessions down the path.

Then I stand up, too, suddenly frightened, feeling like I'm out on the ocean without a life jacket.

I move and walk, and squint the length of Sheridan Road every so often, twirling the car keys in my fingers. Want to see and feel the memory of asphalt that stayed black for a long time, and clean, unworn white lines. A smattering of cars. People walking slowly on the sidewalks. But I can't bring it back.

And in a month or two the sidewalks will throb with bladers, bicycles, skateboards, all zooming toward the pedestrians. It'll be impossible to picture it by then.

So when did they build Dominick's? How did we shop without such a supermarket, anyway? What was on that lot before? And how many times in the last thirty years did I pass through here too quickly? How many times did I visit a friend here, and say, "Oh, I grew up in this neighborhood." And that would be it.

Still a little frightened, I keep walking. I keep putting the car keys away, then taking them out again.

A half-hour has gone by. I'm six blocks farther north, at the corner of Thorndale and Winthrop, right in front of the yard at Swift Grammar School. It looks the same and yet it doesn't. Much smaller yard. The parking lot, the El tracks--so close.

The drugstore is still across the street. God! That day when Mom caught me downing a chocolate malt over there. "What are you doing here, Donna?" she shouted, in front of everyone. "Tonight is Passover! You're supposed to be *home*, helping me set the table, do last minute things." I can still feel the grip of her hands on my shoulders as she steered me out of there. What year was that?

Tonight is Passover, too. Only, it's the nineties now.

Finally, I head back to the parking lot, walking along Sheridan again. I think of the homes, the old ones along Sheridan, where some of my friends lived. Some were modestly fronted, but had spacious insides. Some had wide cement steps leading up to massive wooden doors, which we thought, as kids, must lead to palatial drawing rooms. Ballrooms, too, we thought. We didn't live on Sheridan, but had a big apartment on a tree-lined sidestreet, one block west. We could go out at any hour if we wanted. Sleep at the beach. Nobody bothered you.

I approach the car, touch the door, and the alarm goes off. I groan, fumble with the remote buttons, stop the noise. After I check that the packages are still in back, I decide not to get in. Can't get in yet. I lock the door again, head toward the crowds on the sidewalk.

My cell phone rings. I jump, then grope in my bag for it--not used to this thing yet.

"Where the hell are you, Donna?" my husband Larry asks me.

"Out," I say, almost bumping into a dark-haired girl with a jewel fastened to the side of her nose. "Just out."

"Well, come back, dolly. We're supposed to be at the Seder in two hours."

We are going to his brother's for the traditional dinner. But we are such a small family now at holiday gatherings. Makes me sad sometimes that I was an only child, and that Steve has just the one brother. Our parents are gone.

"Did you call Elaine?" he asks.

"Yes, from work. They sent her home from the hospital. False labor."

Elaine, my child, you're too far away. You're in San Francisco. Why are you having your first baby so far away?

"Give me a little more time," I say.

"Donna!"

"I'm doing something."

A pause. "Hey, Donna what's wrong?"

"I'll be home soon, okay? I won't even change."

Too many people now, I'm thinking.
Loose laces, more earrings on the guys than
the gals. That's everywhere, though. But
the people in business suits, good leather
shoes, expensive jewelry can live up here very
well, cheaper than they could downtown or on
the Gold Coast. And, some of the elderly on
fixed incomes can still get by here.

It's not the inner city--not the cocoon-
like suburbs. An in-between place, built on
the rubble of my memories. With barbed wire
and lots of fences behind the hi-rises.

Built on my memories.

A week ago, it was even worse. I took
a bus up here.

That day I stood across the street from
where the hotel's semicircular driveway used
to be. Well, I'm not sure anymore if it was
a semicircle. A portico? Or a canopy for
people to walk through to the front entrance?
I had scoured my basement for pictures of
the hotel. I knew they were somewhere, but
none surfaced. I could only find grainy, old
newspaper photos.

There was a soldier, though. Him, I
remember. If I close my eyes, I see him
resting his foot on the running board of a
convertible. It had just stopped raining.
A blond was at the wheel of the car, and
her rain-soaked skirt was pulled up slightly
over her knees. I stood there, sweltering
humidity making my sundress stick to me.
Couldn't stop looking. She seemed so worldly,
with her hair in a long wave over one side

133

of her face. Like Veronica Lake. And him?
I'd get so proud, so emotional, whenever I'd
see a serviceman.

Will this war ever end?

My best friend Janice would invite me
to play tennis there, swim in the outdoor
pool. But the grown-ups danced under the
stars. Like being at a Spanish villa--an
estate. We were lucky. All within the city,
in our neighborhood yet.

It's Friday. Cold, but sunny.

I can't believe I'm here again. This
time I went to a Swedish restaurant on Clark
Street. That part of the neighborhood is
called Andersonville. This time I didn't
wander. I ate and came right here.

I should be home, packing to go to San
Francisco. Elaine gave birth last night.
A preemie, he is. Well, three weeks these
days is not really premature. She's named
him Jason, after my father. God! Our first
grandchild. One-day-old Jason.

I didn't sleep all night. I'm zonked,
but so excited. By ten this morning I had
to tell my boss that I needed to leave early
because of the strain. He said, "Just go,
do what you need to do." I'm flying out on
Sunday if I can get a standby. I'll drive
it I have to.

But instead of going straight home, I
go to the park. One more time. Once more,
before I go out to see Jason.

I try to picture him. Who does he look
like? Elaine said his hair is dark, like

our side of the family. Will it fall out, though? Who will he look like as he grows up? When he is grown up?

I feel pulled to the water now. Have to walk east on Bryn Mawr, which bisects Sheridan. And before I go under the Outer Drive overpass, to go to the lake, I stop, look at the one remaining building from my hotel memories--a tall, pale pink, X-shaped apartment building. An anchor at the north end of the complex. At the end of where the complex used to be.

Daddy liked that building. Always studying its style.

Then I climb over grass that hasn't come up yet, cross the running path, the bike path, and finally make it to the step-rocks that rim Lake Michigan here. No bag ladies anywhere. Just the smell of pot wafting around, lingering, probably from the group of guys down to the right, who are crouching in front of the first step.

And back across the Drive, the condos loom above the strip of park where I sat Wednesday.

Up high, in a lot of those apartments, you can look out over the curves and points of the shoreline and see it wind its way toward downtown. See curved strings of lights at night. Harbors, bike paths, running paths, and the golf course come into view during the day. Gridlock you don't always see. Your eyes go to the shoreline, and the parks alongside.

My eyes shoot back to the pink building--the only thing that miraculously escaped the demolishing.

The yellow walls of the hotel loomed up ahead of us that day.

"Daddy, Daddy!"

He smiled at me, brushed my red-brown bangs off my forehead, took my hand.

"C'mon, Daddy. We'll miss our stop."

Uncle Harry was waiting at the hotel, had taken a room there, and we were going inside, probably to lunch with him. We'd see pictures of Aunt Edna, who was always ailing and couldn't ever make the trip. We'd see pictures of my cousins. We'd hear about Uncle Harry's latest business trips--of which this was one.

Wait! Did the bus go this far in the forties? Yes. Well, didn't it? Or did we take a cab? No. A cab all the way back from our cleaning store on the South Side?

But, Daddy didn't drive anymore, and the car sat parked at the curb. So when I went to visit him in the store, Mama took me. She used the car sometimes, mostly to shop, to pick up fish or fruits and vegetables, or to go to a farmer's stand in Lincolnwood or Skokie. When I'd come along, I'd try to get a slice of watermelon, or a lemonade, and sit on the running board, sweating, hoping to cool myself. If Daddy went with, he'd sit in the shade and look sad.

Too cold out here now. Twenties and thirties in April? Possible snow flurries? At Passover?

I watch a few bicycles zip by. Some go along the step in front of me: one goes along the slab closest to a whitecapped Lake Michigan.

Gotta go home and pack. I get up and start back. On the way, I see the ribbon of traffic starting; then, the fences behind the buildings. I force myself to picture the air and sky that was here before the buildings. Can't.

I plunk down on another cold bench, one down from where the bag lady and I were, I think. A gust of winter-like wind hits me in the face. I'm thinking how Larry must be worried about me.

As I go into my purse for the phone to call him, I see a little child in a green parka ride by on his tricycle. He rolls it into the grass and stops.

The sight of him starts me crying. My numbed, cold limbs are shaking. Suddenly, I think of Jason. Then Daddy. What's going on?

The kid turns, stares at me.

"This is where I came." It just tumbles out of me, then scares me. "This *must* be where I came."

First the kid is still. Then he starts to twist around, looking for someone.

"This is where I came the night he died."

A woman in tight jeans and a short leather jacket runs toward the kid, plants a hand on his shoulder, gives him a quick spank on his rear.

Tears flood my face now. All I could think of, when they took him away, was to run. To come here. "It--it must have been here. Or very close to here."

Larry knows this. Mom guessed, I'm sure. I never told anyone else. But now I start to feel it. How it must have been.

Not even sure who took him away, who took my daddy away. Or how long I stayed here. Just that I left her. Deserted my mom!

"The old geezer probably had a heart attack," the paramedics said as they came up the steps to our apartment that day. Even at age eleven I knew that a forty-nine-year-old man was not an "old geezer." I cried and cried. And later I ran . . .

I put my red, cold fingers over my eyes now. "Oh, my God!"

The woman and the kid stare at me.

"Oh, God," is all I can say.

She hasn't moved. But she looks like she might come closer.

I lower my head, focus on the ground below.

Finally, she says to the kid, "Shush. This is not a place to cry."

I don't look up, but out of the corner of my eye, I see them take off. See them take the path that once was at water's edge.

For what seems like a very long time, I sit, knees locked, shoulders clenched. Trying, trying now to picture the couples, how they strolled arm in arm. This time, they move under a night sky. They dance under the stars.

I want to think of Mom and Dad, before it ended, before that terrible day.

They came here in the thirties, before I was born, too. They might've had dinner right behind me here. In the Marine Dining room? They might've sat right here, even back when they were dating. This slightly cracked sidewalk has taken the place of the Beachwalk they talked about.

They sat right here, of course, long before I ever did, facing the water. Mom and Dad--young, laughing, planning a future. And I'm so comforted by that scene. The two of them, sitting, talking about a life together. Talking about dreams. Most of them, dreams that would never come true.

I should tell Jason about it. About the good things. Of course. I *will* tell him about it. Tell him about me, too. What his Gramma Donna was like when she was little. He should know about his great grandparents, and the old neighborhood, too. Have to keep it going. Keep it connected.

He'll think I'm silly when I talk about the hotel, about the sunlight and the moonlight and the beautiful people from another age. I'll make it a good story, though. I'll try.

I stand up. One leg is asleep, both are numb from the cold. My mind, my whole body, is weak from tripping back and forth between the forties and the nineties. I start to walk. I won't think so hard anymore. I'm old now, and I'm little again, too, and all the years in between have gone away for a while.

Soon, my legs unstiffen. I am hurrying back to the car, anxious to be with my husband now. So anxious to hold my grandson for the first time.

WOMANCHILD

I sat facing Dr. Carlson across the large expanse of polished mahogany desktop. We were about to go over yet another medical report about me, and I couldn't stand it. Not another time. My mind started to drift, then jump ahead: in two hours I'd be sitting in class. It gave me comfort, gave me back some dignity.

A fifty-year-old girl, in school again. Temporarily insulated from the world I'd been thrown into after the divorce.

I tried to pay attention to Carlson, but soon I was dancing between listening and spacing out, tunnel-visioning to today's class at the School for Design.

In that class--in the whole building--I was still a person instead of a "case history." I might've been a person with a weak leg and numb fingers, who felt very self-conscious about it these days, but inside that building, the feeling almost went away. There, I felt creative. I could finally be myself and make something out of my life.

Dr. Carlson took off his glasses, rubbed his white mustache.

"Stacie," he said to me, "you're a difficult case."

"Look, something's wrong. Why can't they find it?"

"They didn't say there's nothing--"

"Hey, it's like they're *looking* for nothing to be wrong."

141

"Two of them said your responses on exam were abnormal," he said, "that it's probably a conduction defect. The MRI did show an abnormality, but it wasn't definitive." He smiled weakly, shifted his weight in the worn, black leather chair. "No actual lesions or tumors to correlate with...your symptoms. Well, this report calls it a `myelopathy', says the defect is mild, minimal."

"Minimal."

"You have to get on with your life, Stacie."

"Tripping over your toes is minimal."

No answer.

"Not being able to step on the gas, hit the brake fast, or even squeeze it, I suppose that's minimal, too."

I should be doing this better, I thought. Last night I pushed shampoo into my ear, couldn't feel how to hold my hair in my right hand. Don't you get it, Carlson?

What did I look like to him now? Inarticulate, too-thin woman, with a net of fine lines around her green eyes, and a crop of fuzzy gray and honey-streaked hair gathered at the nape of her neck with an old scarf covered in a hot-air-balloon pattern. But, if this was Peggy here today--Peggy, my lawyer-sister--she would demand he do something. First my leg and now my hand?

"...make the most of it, live with it." Carlson's chubby behind squished into the chair, and there was no smile on his ruddy face now.

This round may be over, I thought.

142

So I shouted, "I can't keep it going like this."

A gentle knock on the door stopped me. His nurse Ruth pushed it half open and said that a doctor in the emergency room was calling on the house line.

He looked at me and sighed. I crimped my mouth at him. "All right, Ruth, I'll take it in the other office."

After he was gone a couple of minutes, I got up and went to the window. Men and women in white coats, and a few construction workers, dotted the sun-splashed sidewalk below. A line had formed at the coffee and snack wagon. More minutes passed. Where was he? I waited, watched a couple wearing backpacks scuttle across the flower-lined esplanade on the right, grab an empty bench. I could see an elevated train slowing to a stop at the platform a block away. Still, he didn't return.

Then I came back to the desk, leaned over, and carefully slid the report around.

Reading fast, it was a blur of narrative, peppered with test results. Blood tests, nerve conduction studies, and MRI scans. Familiar words and medical phrases appeared: patient "presents"; and, patient "denies"; and patient has a "constellation" of symptoms. But something on the last page jumped out at me:

"Ms. Hellman should strongly consider psychiatric intervention."

It was like I'd been hit. For a minute I didn't know who they were talking about.

But it was me, of course. Talking like they knew me. The dumb bastards, like they really knew me. "Intervention"? I knew the tests weren't going to show much, but even so...

Oh, God, the questions. What had I said to that doctor? What answers did I give to that paled-faced girl with the rimless glasses who made me look at pictures, play with puzzle parts, fill out a long questionnaire?

Finally, I closed the report, pushed it back to his side.

When Carlson and I were face to face again, I couldn't talk. He just squeezed his eyes shut and opened them extra wide at me. "Stacie, you are a difficult case."

I took a deep breath. My mouth was dry, like I'd rinsed with chalk-water.

"You're upset now," he said, "with Mother in the hospital."

"No. I'm `upset now' because I'm tired, and this thing is getting worse. And the--the `psychiatric' crap, what's that all about?"

He lifted an eyebrow. It got quiet again. I was reaching now, didn't know how to do what I wanted to do anymore. What a joke. Neither of us knew what to do.

We went back so far, Carlson and us. Peggy and I had met him when we were teenagers and he was a skinny, vigorous thirty-year-old. For years, I could always tell him anything, thought he knew everything. But this new weakness had changed me, and a hysterectomy three years earlier had changed me, and three years of doctors had really changed me. And lately, talking to him felt like we were having a business meeting, where I wanted to protect myself.

He put the glasses back on. "Now, we've been to at least three . . . yes, three neurologists, and two orthopedic specialists."

"We?"

"Some think it's neurological," he said, "possibly multiple sclerosis. Others, orthopedic."

Don't do this anymore, I thought. You'll have a stroke. But suddenly, my anger was receding, slipping away. Going to some place inside where it could no longer be expressed so badly, in so unfocused a way. Why did it always end up like this?

"All right," I said, quietly, feeling we'd done the scene before. "I *am* getting on with my life. Finishing school. But I live with Mom, take care of her. And I'm losing my strength. And it's been a hell of a summer."

A hell of a summer. The nightmarish end of having to move in with her five years earlier because I couldn't keep driving back and forth from one suburb to another. I had never belonged there, even before her cancer. What had started as a good deed became an after-divorce refuge for me.

Carlson placed his hands over my now-closed file. "You can't keep taking tests. You *can*, but you may never get an answer."

145

"They wouldn't treat a man this way.   A man would be pissed."

He laughed.

"And you know it as well as I do," I said.

"Just don't go doctor-shopping, Stacie."

I slid forward in the chair, reached down for my tote bag, my fold-up cane, then looked him in the eye.   "I have to get to my eleven o'clock class."

ROLLING HOME

"Who is that woman in the mirror? Who is she?"

Today I really mean it. Now that I have to sit so much, I see her a lot. I look more like her than ever.

All I was doing was admiring the view out the window here. Such a pretty streetscape--plants and flowers along that brick path, the cute iron benches. Thick grass, too. Even the tall buildings, like the one I'm in, are bright, splashed with sun today. And the new museum, and the almond-colored stone walls of the old water tower pumping station--all so pretty. Such a pretty scene.

But when I swung my eyes back inside, I did see the hairdresser's tools, sure, and the high chair I was sitting in--and I saw her, too.

Look at her thighs. My God. Never put them in shorts, or even culottes, again. Everything sagging now. Cover her up.

"Who is she?"

"What, dear?" my hairdresser asks.

"Nothing," I answer. "Nothing."

Is her face on my shoulders? It looks younger than my body. But very pale, with mask-like features, like my mother's the year she died. When I start to smile I crimp the corners of my mouth and tilt my brows like she did.

But today my face should be pink, from the facial I just had. The pink flush has gone away already, and the paintbrush-thin

147

eyebrows, well, I can't get used to them yet. Even though I asked for "thin", I'm scared of the look.

"We should cut it shorter," he says, holding up a section of nearly all gray hair at the top of my head. Holds the hair between his fingers and points with the other hand. "Shape the neckline a little, blend it in," he says. "Shorter for summer. Boy, it really grew while you were in the hospital."

What about the bald spots by my temples? How will "we" cover them? In the hospital they looked bad no matter how I combed it.

So hard to talk to him today...and chase her away, too. If I don't act right, he'll think he can do whatever he wants with me. Like that guy in that other beauty shop, two years ago. A smart aleck in a blue suit, and such a dark shirt, with an earring in his ear. He tells me, "Mrs. Johnson, you don't know what you want."

My friends, even my son Harold, said to let it go. Only a joke. I didn't let it go. First, I was ashamed, then I made them sorry. I stayed away from there for a long time, and when I came back I went to another hairdresser, a woman instead, and he kept asking me how I was and if he could get me coffee...

In the beginning, she looked just like my mom--dishwater-blond hair tied in a bun at the nape of her neck, big breasts tucked into the one-piece corset she wore. A couple of times she was dying, mouth gaping like a flattened doughnut, hair stuck to the pillow with sweat. Some days, I don't know her at all.

I talk only to the psychiatrist about her. He's the only one. Even to him, I'm ashamed.

I look straight into the big mirror, then to the side mirror on the right. "Timothy, leave some hair around my face, and ears. Okay? Please. I don't want my ears showing."

He smiles and continues cutting. "No problem. I think I'll give you a half-bang, with a little flip. Do it to the side instead of all back."

I tell him fine. He keeps snipping until it's time for the gels and lotions and the blowdryer. I don't have it set in rollers anymore because I can't stand the sound of the dryer.

I'm not crazy: I know it's me. Most of the time. But sometimes I want to run from her. But I can hardly walk, so how could I get away? Sometimes, though, when I've upset people, or made them really angry, I get scared and imagine she wants to kill me for it.

All of a sudden Verona is walking toward me with my coffee. No, not Verona. That was the other place. This woman is lovely and makes such good coffee. I take the cup, but wish I could go into the dressing room with her, right now, and tell her how miserable I am.

My hands shake as I lift the cup to my lips: a creepy feeling is coming over me. I see the scissors lying on a towel on the top shelf of the hairdresser's cart. I wonder what it would be like to pick them up, put them near my face...

I look down at my lap. "Harold is coming by for me," I tell them. "My son. We're getting to be such good friends lately."

"That's neat," Timothy says. "You're lucky."

"I know. He's my only baby."

If I sip my coffee, chat with them, it will all be over soon.

It is a half-hour later and I am dressed in my blue linen slacks and white nylon blouse, the blouse with the ruffles down the front. I want to get out of here now but I sit in my wheelchair, keep my hands carefully draped across the jacket in my lap. Don't mess the nails, I'm thinking.

Oh, I think I see her! Near my chair. No. No, I don't.

But Harold is here. At the reception counter, just a few feet away, paying my bill. Good. I told Verona, or that other lady, to push me up there so I could do it myself. Harold always wants to treat me, even though I got more money than he does. See, today is my birthday, and the lady who takes care of me has the day off because Harold and I are going out for dinner tonight, anyway.

Finally we're finished, and everyone is telling me how nice I look and we are all saying goodbye.

As we wait for the elevator I feel a little better. She's like, hiding somewhere. Harold and I are alone here. Now I don't know who's younger, who's older.

"To think I used to schlep you around like this, Harold."

"I'm sure I loved it, darling. I can almost remember."

I turn my head toward him. "No. No, you can't. Can you?"

"Sure, Ma."

"Did you know that before you were born, honey, Daddy and I used to sing a lot?"

"I know, Ma."

"I sang to you, too, when you were little."

I try to remember the lines from old songs, operettas. They mix up in my head. Just when I do remember something, the elevator door opens and people rush out. Next time I'll sing.

Down in the lobby we stop at a marble bench so I can look in my purse for a scarf--the real thin, oblong one. Peach color, I think. Can't find it. All that's in here is a heavy, blue one. Folded up tight, and wrinkled. This one's slippery.

I feel like crying. Crying like I did in the hospital when they were helping me to walk and Harold was next to me and I couldn't hold on to the metal railing in that practice place.

Tears well up in my eyes. "If it hadn't been for the stroke, I'd look...feel so good

now. Maybe...maybe I'd be out running or
something. Or skiing."

He comes to the front of me, takes my
hand. "That's right, Ma. You'd be the one
to go off skiing. Hell, you taught me."

"I'm slipping."

"You're not slipping. We're going to
make you better. We're going to do the best
we can."

"I am. It's too fast."

He has such green eyes. Takes after
me. Dark blond hair. I'm imagining how
that hair hasn't changed much and we could
be on another bench, right here, and it could
be forty years ago. Harold liked to build
castles in the playground sandlot. Such
shapes he made. With only a green pail and
shovel. I'd take an old spoon or pencil and
help make windows and doors.

"Remember the playground, Harold?"

"Sure," he says.

It was on the east side of Michigan
Avenue, here, where this building is. And
there were tennis courts in the next block
that you couldn't see from the street because
a billboard protected them from the busy
sidewalk. I think that's how it was. I
won't say it. Maybe I have it wrong.

He stands up, rises to his full six-
foot-three height. "Okay, let's roll. Time
to get going, let you rest before dinner."

I want to tell you, Harold. I'm getting
so scared of her.

No. Talk to the doctor next week.

I say nothing. We go out the double doors--the sliding doors that wheelchairs have to use.

Outside the street is filled with people, cabs, busses. We wait for the light alongside an older couple who are both wearing jackets over jeans. They have weathered skin. The man is balding, but sporting a ponytail. I try to picture Harold like that. He is so neat. Even his roommate John is so neat. But I won't say a word if one day I see ponytails, or earrings.

When we get across the street I ask, "Harold, can we sit here, in front of the Hancock? For a few minutes?"

He says yes, and I know he likes the noonday crowds, the people-watching as much as I do. So he parks my chair alongside one of the square cement-rimmed planters. You can sit on the foot-deep rim and watch the bodies criss-cross the Hancock Plaza. Today, water is swishing up the fountain wall on the lower level, and music is playing.

I'm much happier now.

Soon, a group of four people, carrying shopping bags from Crate and Barrel, and Niketown stop in front of us. "Can you go up to the top?" one of them asks. "Which entrance is it?"

Harold gives them directions, tells them they can have lunch up there, too, in the restaurant below the Observatory floor.

"They have a wonderful buffet," I add. "Reasonable." I feel very helpful now, wish

I had a map or something. Wish I had a CTA map so I could tell them how to take busses to places where the natives go. After all, isn't this my territory? My old neighborhood. Where it was so quiet on Sundays, compared to now, and restaurants were hidden in buildings and the most exciting thing was to sit in the Drake Hotel lobby.

After they leave, I glance down the row of trees that are in planters like the one we are at. Two away from where we are, another wheelchair sits. A white-haired man, with head bent over and knees covered by a white blanket, sits motionless. His companion, a tall woman in a white uniform, keeps tucking and adjusting the blanket around him carefully.

I watch, looking for signs of life, a little animation. Anything. I know Harold is looking, too. We don't speak.

We are gliding north, down Michigan Avenue, going toward my apartment. I see shop windows of that building Bloomingdale's is in, the Drake Hotel on the other side of the street. I like this part, don't feel conspicuous, even in the chair. But we are both thinking of that man. I know I am. If he *was* a man.

We get to Oak street, where Michigan Avenue ends and Lake Shore Drive will take over. Oak Street beach comes into view, and the eight lanes of Outer Drive traffic that parallel it can't steal it's brilliance.

Our neighborhood. Sun on water. The sand castles you used to build there, Harold. And before that, your dad, and a very pregnant me, used to walk along that sand.

Two blocks later, I feel relaxed, safe. "Harold?"

"Yeah?"

"I have something to tell you."

He slows down. "A quick thing, or an after-dinner thing."

"It's important, honey," I say.

He stops walking, comes around in front of me.

"Now, don't worry, Harold. But it *is* complicated. So, for sure, it'll be an over-dinner thing."

LIKE LOOKING FOR FIRE ENGINES

It felt like stage fright--but the good kind, where the excitement of what you're going to do is bigger than how scared you are. My heart was pounding, but I couldn't wait to talk to him, so I didn't go up to my locker first. I dialed his office from the lobby.

He answered before the second ring. "David Chapman." His voice was businesslike, and slightly dulled.

"Hi," I said. "It's Karyn."

"Karyn." A pause. "Oh, hi."

"I got the tickets. Is Sunday too soon? Sunday at four? They don't have anything on a Friday or Saturday for a while."

"No? Uh, fine. Great. Who're we going to see?"

"Surprise. It will be down in Merrillville, like I said. You know, down in Indiana? But don't look for it in the paper."

"Okay, I'm in your hands." Another pause. I heard him take in a deep breath. "It's at four?"

Here it comes, I thought. I can still get out of it, suggest we play it by ear, see how we feel after the concert. "Karyn? It's at four?"

"Yeah."

Did he remember what I'd said? About "some of us old folks getting sleepy on the ride home"?

"So, we have to eat dinner," he said. "Why drive back to Chicago right away?"

"Good idea," I said. "Well, do you want to have dinner and then..." My heart started to pound again. "Think we should stay over? I mean, can you?"

He answered me fast. "Yes, I can, and I want to."

So we decided I'd come downtown and stay with my sister Anita and he wouldn't have to go way up north to my house before we headed back south to Merrillville. But where was he coming from? His house in the burbs? And how was he getting away from her, for God sakes?

I offered my car, offered to drive.

"Oh, I don't mind driving," he said. "But if I break a bone, you could get us back, right?"

"Sure. All I need is cruise, in case my bad leg gets tired."

He said he'd call me Saturday night. I told him that if Anita answered and asked who was calling he should give his middle name--which he now told me was Aaron. Just in case. "Well," he said hesitantly, "then I'll check on the motels down there? Surprise you?"

"Okay. A lot of surprises." Then I remembered I'd have to tell Anita something about where I'd be. "Oh, wait. I'll tell her a bunch of us are going to meet and all go down together, and that I may stay over at a girlfriend's house. Otherwise, she'll ask what motel I'm at."

"Sounds pretty good." I heard him let out a breath. "Karyn? I'm really looking forward to it. A bad week ahead. It's going to be a bad week."

Are they getting a divorce? I wondered. What bad week? A bad week at work?

I gave him directions and Anita's number, then told him not to pull into the driveway. He gave me his phone number. It had a suburban area code. I wasn't supposed to use it unless an emergency came up.

He must still be living with her, I thought. Am I a nut for doing this? Am I just a fifty-year-old student who's dumb enough to think she can go away with her teacher and pull it off?

Sunday morning. At dawn, a red-yellow sunrise; afterwards, a clear blue, cloudless sky promising a crisp autumn day.

I awoke at sunrise. For an hour I must've opened and closed my eyes a dozen times, trying to make sleep come back, but it wouldn't. David was picking me up at one-thirty, and I wanted to sleep as late as possible. But the last time I opened my eyes, the white alarm clock on the nightstand said only 8:30, and I still hadn't gone back to sleep. I lay there, warm, still floating in that receding-from-the-world sensation of dozing and waking, daydreaming about the evening.

No more than twenty minutes could've passed after I'd looked at the time, when something jolted me. Pulsating, unexplainable fear. Nauseating. First it was like the panic you feel when you think your wallet is gone. Then it was like quicksand or lead blankets were holding me down. Still too groggy to figure out exactly what it was, I was sure something worse was going to happen next.

"Anita!" My cry sounded weak, like when you try to yell in a bad dream and little comes out. "Anita? Oh, God! Anita!"

When she didn't appear, I sat up. By then my heart was racing in irregular, staccato beats under my ribs. When I tried to stand up, I fell back down, but was surprised and relieved I could move at all. My body was hot, burning. But at least I had moved, even though my hands and feet still felt heavy. I shook my hands hard and stood up again. My right leg was dragging a little, but I could stamp the left one up and down, move my tingly wrists back and forth. I kept shaking everything. Hard. I stumbled to the door, and staggered out into the hall.

Then I remembered that Anita's friend Lynn was staying over, in Anita's room. Their door was closed.

Air. Maybe there hadn't been enough cool air during the night. But the window had been open, all night. I kept pushing myself down the hall. The terrace. Go out and breathe more fresh air. Or, lie down flat like you're supposed to do when you're feeling faint.

But by then, except for a mild buzz just under my skin, everything was going away--fast. All the frightening sensations--gone as fast as they had come.

Now the fear of why it happened set in, and the fear that it might happen again.

I slid the terrace door wide open and sat at the dining room table, still alert for signs that it might start over.

They say you're supposed to think about something else, I told myself, anything but your body, when you feel sick like that. They say when you have a bad heart valve like I do you can panic like that. Bad spine, bad heart. Who knows, I thought, running my hands over the honey-colored, birchwood tabletop. Okay. Let's see. Country furniture here. Farm furniture. Santa Fe influence. Anita's house was an eclectic mix. We'd picked most of it out together at the Merchandise Mart showroom back in the early eighties.

I stroked the green antique stain on the legs of the table, and thought about what a ball we'd had putting it all together. I thought about what shampoo I'd use today, how pretty the new sweater I was going to wear tonight looked. I thought about whether I should squeeze oranges for breakfast or open a carton.

Then, more thoughts. Like bullets. What was going to happen tonight? How fast do we move? Who starts what? And, how could a fifty-year-old woman not know?

Maybe I'd do just as bad with him as I had with Danny.

I clenched my hands thinking about Danny. But at least he'd been my age. David must be under forty. At least, back then I didn't have the bad leg. But still it hadn't worked. And only a year after the divorce, he got married again. This time it was to a fetus--a fetus who hopefully would keep her two good legs healthy.

Words popped into my head now: "If you're going to act like this again, we should just end this thing!"

Danny had said that as we lay there in our large, sunny hotel room in the Bahamas. Ten years ago. Back from the pool, and in bed, instead of getting ready to go to dinner.

I started to cry, and every time he brought his face close to me, my shakes added to the tears.

"You just stop, Karyn!"

"Honey, it comes and goes, takes time." Tears rolled down my cheeks. I was afraid, but knew he'd stop eventually.

"You were looking off in space, trying to push me away. Goddamn it! Then you lay there and start to squirm..."

"I don't like--"

"You don't like any of it unless you've got two martinis in you."

"Please, Danny,"--I put my knees together and pulled the sheet over me-- "people will hear."

"What is it you don't like?" He jumped out of bed, reached for a cigarette, and stood in front of the dresser, looking down at me. "You like the money we have now, and the big house, and doing nothing all day."

"Nothing?"

"God, it takes you all morning to get ready to go out to lunch."

"I just don't like it when you..."

"When I what?" he yelled. "What? Go down on you?"

"Stop."

"Can't you even say it? Or do you need a drink? Maybe we should parade you out by the pool, or go to the bar for a while."

"I said stop it!"

"How long will it take? Will two be enough?" But it didn't come out of him like a question--at least not one he wanted an answer for.

"I hate--it doesn't feel right. And then...then your mouth tastes like it's from me. Why do you have to make me feel so bad."

"Most women would love it." He flung the cigarette, and the whole pack, against the wall. "Your mom really did a number on you. She really messed you up."

I know there's something wrong with me, I kept saying over and over. Something wrong with me.

"Maybe we should just end this thing now," he said.

I panicked. Would he do that? Leave me? "I know there's something wrong with me.

163

I'll try harder. I love you." Carefully, I'd repeated it over and over--something wrong with me, something wrong with me...

But soon he was calming down, and he was comforting me like a parent does a child, and we went out to dinner that night, tanned and bright-eyed, looking happy--a couple everyone in the dining room must have admired...

Maybe there still was something wrong, and I really was a nut to think I could pull it off with David.

I played with the edges of the woven placemats on the table. Finally, I got up and went into the kitchen, decided to start breakfast, even though they weren't up yet.

I ran the cold water for coffee a good three minutes, inserted the paper cone in the coffeemaker, and poured in the special breakfast blend Anita used--which had already been measured and ground, and put in a tiny plastic bag.

After I pushed the switch and heard the hiss-drip start, I looked in the fridge for fruit or juice. Anita hated carton juice, and there wasn't anything already squeezed, so the choice was between melon, oranges, and the bananas lying on the white Corian countertop. I pulled six oranges from the crisper drawer.

As I closed the refrigerator door, oranges cradled in my arms, the buzzy sensation returned. I started to slice the oranges carefully, praying that slow,

deliberate movements would make the rest of
me slow down, too.

"Karyn?"

I jumped, turned to see Lynn in the
doorway. Three oranges tumbled away from me,
rolled off the counter and into the corner.

"God, you scared me." Too soon, I
thought, I want to be alone a little longer.
"Guess I'm all thumbs today. These people,
they've never...been to a Country concert."
I picked up the oranges from the floor.

"Feel responsible, huh?" she asked. A
wedge of curly, gray-brown hair fell across
her cheekbone as she took spoons out of the
drawer.

"Yeah, right. What if they hate it?"

"It'll be fine," she said. "Oh, we
have croissants and honey bran muffins in the
fridge."

I plugged in the juicer and lined up
the oranges again on paper towels. "Juice
and coffee's all I want now." A tinge of
queasiness rose in my throat as I sliced them
in half.

*I can't go through with it. Of course,
I can't.* I'll have to call him.

"...got a lot to do today," Lynn was
saying as she set out spoons, knives, and
mugs on the place mats at the table.

"You're having company?" I asked.

"Eight people for dinner. And your
sister wants everything just so."

"Drives you crazy, right?"

Maybe I could go through with it, I
thought.

165

"Yes," Lynn said. "We practically interrogated the butcher yesterday. I was so embarrassed. And Jesus, forty-five minutes to pick out veggies. Bread has to be from Jerome's."

"It's good bread." I laughed, all of a sudden feeling a little better. "I thought you knew her by now."

"I do, but will they care where the bread came from, or what glasses we use? She works so hard all week, why--?"

"She wasn't that bad in high school. Something happened about yuppie time. See, we used to be poor. No pot to piss in?" The coffeemaker had stopped and the sharp, nutty aroma of fresh coffee filled the kitchen. I pulled out the wet cone, wadded it around the hot grounds, and threw it in the garbage.

"I know she wants to please people, Karyn, but--"

"The best. She's got a thing about the best. Perfectionism. If it stopped with the cooking or--well, just her work..." I kept my eyes on the juicer as I plunged the orange halves down on the squeezer. "Listen, I could never do anything right for her," I said quietly.

When we sat down with the pitcher of juice and our mugs of coffee, we both fell silent. Since I'd known Lynn I'd been careful not to knock Anita, and I regretted opening my big mouth.

I came down early, at one.

As I stood on the walk just outside the revolving door, I watched a few yellow and orange-red leaves float down lazily from the trees across the street. A small collection dotted the grass and lay ribbon-like at the curbs.

I looked for him, but no David yet.

Then a chilling thought crossed my mind. Next year at this time, I might not be walking. The next time this beauty happens, I might not be walking. The thought focused, really gripped. If things get worse, I could be in one of those little carts, mini motor-scooters. Waiting in line for restaurants and restrooms from a seated position...

What the hell was I doing going away with this guy?

"Need some help?" Art, good doorman that he was, had come sailing out from the lobby. "Need help?"

"Oh, no, thanks." I pointed to my blue weekender sitting on the sidewalk at my feet. "It's not heavy." I picked it up.

Just then I saw David cruising by, his head tilted toward the building.

"I think I see them now, Art. Thanks."

David must have read my mind. He let me throw the bag in the back seat fast, then drove a half block away before we laughed, and said hello. And it was only one-fifteen.

After the concert, I remembered about calling Anita. Most of the phones were busy. So we took the third-floor enclosed walkway out of the theater, then followed some people into the connecting Radisson Hotel. "I gotta call home," I said. "Say, you really enjoyed it. I could tell."

He grinned. "Their voices were--well, it was everything you promised." He laughed. "Not all `my girl left me and my horse ran away' anymore."

"Oh, c'mon." I gave him a mock punch in the chest. "You knew that. Hey, you wondered why I got a headset glued to my ears all the time."

"Okay, I'm impressed."

How was he going to touch me? I wondered. In a fast, take-it-for-granted way? But he wouldn't be here if he didn't care--a little. If he wanted a quickie, or a matinee, he could get anyone. Any time. Didn't have to come down here.

It looked like safari-land in the lobby. Artificially-created rocky walls surrounded a small maze of paths that went past trees, several outpost-type bar areas, and a submerged-in-sand Landrover-type car. A playground, of all things, was also set in sand. Nestled at the bottom of it all, just below walk-in level, was an indoor pool.

"Neat." I pointed to an exotic bird watching over the scene from its perch in a domed cage.

"Different," he said. "Maybe we should've stayed here."

I glanced up at the upper levels, at the rooms that faced inward, with their small, cordoned-off terraces, and tables and chairs.

Then I did something strangely out of form: slipped my arm around his waist, catching his arm as well. I gave him a quick squeeze, and pulled away--feeling close and familiar, as if we'd cased hotel lobbies before, done all this before.

My mind streaked back to that day in his office--his newly decorated office. His face--flushed but tired, and so close to mine. Standing at the window waiting to see fire trucks follow the blaring sirens we'd heard. No fire trucks, though. Air thick with the quietness. Bodies too close, and my skin feeling that tickle, that electricity of almost touching...

We held hands as we walked up to a vacant pay phone, kept them locked as I punched in the numbers for a credit-card call.

Lynn answered on the third ring. "Hello?"

"Hi, it's me. Still down here, and...and one of the girls has a house in Crown Point. I mean, her parents do. So I think I'll stay overnight." I tightened my fingers over his. "We'll take our time coming back tomorrow." I heard noise in the background, laughing and loud voices.

"You have the key, right?"

"Oh, sure."

"What?" she shouted.

"Yes, I have the key," I said louder. "I told Anita where I might stay before I left. Well, see you tomorrow, okay?"

"Sure. Oh! Was the concert good?"

"Great," I told her as I looked into his eyes. "Bye."

We left the Radisson and went to another place to eat.

But during dinner, our conversation lagged. Too much polite small talk. I had a hard time deciding how to act with him.

So I sat there, eating slowly, unprotected by the usual school talk, or any fantasies I could control from the awkward middle back to the fabulous, promising beginning.

Virgin territory now.

"Well," he said, taking a large swallow of his wine. "You know I'm separated. I guess I should tell you--"

"No, no. You don't have to."

He went on as if I hadn't said anything. "Nancy and I, we're separated. Sort of. She's gone back to Boston, that's where we used to live. My parents are there, too."

I should stop him, I thought, concentrating hard on slicing off another crusty slab of bread. I twirled the crumbs around on the bread board with my knife.

"...but our backgrounds were different, very different."

What was "different", I thought.

"It's okay, David. I mean, I'm--you don't have to explain."

"So if I'd kept my mouth shut, pretended this was just--"

"I'm here, and I didn't...really know you were separated. But I didn't ask, either, did I?"

Later, after the waiter took our empty dessert plates away and left the check, I poured us another cup of coffee. "Would you have? Gone if things were okay?"

"No," he said. "But, none of it's like me, though."

"Well, it's not like me, either." I leaned closer to the table. "You know, I found ways to bump into you a lot, but then I'd worry about how funny my walking looked and lose my nerve." He smiled at that.

"And once, I saw you talking to your secretary? in that temporary office when they were fixing yours? Well, you were laughing with her, and I was about to `bump' into you, but I got so jealous."

A slight blush crept up his cheeks. "I was nervous, too, whenever I'd bump into you. Even in class."

"Yeah?"

"And you always sat in the front row. I just had a feeling about you. I thought I had the idea first."

"Oh?" I gazed around the country-lodge decor of the restaurant--wood paneling, dark swirl-patterned carpet, polished wood chairs, tables covered with crisp linen cloths. Everything seemed so perfect. "It might be too much for me to live up to, this idea." I looked into his dark brown eyes. Then, for all the tension I had felt, I couldn't see past him, as if we were the only ones having dinner in that room. Nancy could've been in the next room.

He leaned forward, put his elbow on the table and pressed two curled fingers under his chin.

I saw the space where his wedding should have been.

"You try to be flip," he said. "Sometimes you're serious. Angry, too."

"Angry? Boy, I hope that's not it." A wave of heat shot through me. I could smell the perfume I was wearing drifting up from my sweater, from the hair behind my ears. For a moment, the bad leg wasn't there.

"Karyn, one minute you're cool, then there's this--I don't know--nervous edge. Makes *me* a little nervous."

"Nervous is good. That's a seduction already."

"And standing so long looking for fire engines? What was that?"

I blushed. The memory of standing at that window brought a another rush of heat down my spine.

"Would you like a drink?" he asked back at our motel.

We'd explored the game room, empty party-rooms, corridors, the gift shop windows--even the grounds outside--and it wasn't even ten o'clock yet.

"Go back home, Karyn?"

"Neither."

"I brought a bottle of wine." His hand shook a couple of times as he reached into his pocket for the key.

"That's nice," I told him, moving closer.

INTO THE NIGHT

Just because you're over seventy doesn't mean the doctor should keep you waiting while he talks to a young babe who's worried she may never run again.

Well, I think that's what's going on. See, first they plopped me in this examining room, and then, in the middle of everything, Doctor had to step out for a minute. Already, I can't remember why he left. Anyway, he left the door half-open, and all of a sudden I'm seeing them standing together..

I see his short dark hair, tan neck, the crisp white coat and the khaki, crepe-soled shoes he is wearing. I gawk at the high, small boobs on her that don't need even the tanktop she's wearing to keep them in place. Jesus. And long, blond-streaked hair, above golden-brown, muscled legs. No, only one muscled leg. The other is in a full cast. Still, she is a gazelle.

I used to be a gazelle, too. No, no. More like a horse. Raising four kids, waitressing on weekends so they could get their orthodonture and their piano lessons and their dance lessons. Back then, before we had a little money in the bank. A horse.

Well, I talked to her already, in the waiting room. Her, in this cast, crutches resting neatly against the nearby chair. A boyfriend, holding a wad of keys in his hand, looking at her so attentively. And me? Sitting obediently behind my walker, the

175

one with the collapsible seat and small bag hanging in the front.

And Max? my dear husband? He was looking for a sports magazine. Looking at his watch, too. (Doctor was running late.) "Hope we'll be home in time to watch Jeopardy," Max said.

So I told him not to come into the room with me. Next time I'll tell him to stay home altogether. Yeah. Like he really wants to play the game anymore. Like he wouldn't really want to be with the other retired friends, the other old cockers. Only semi-retired, though, Max is.

I mean, there have been so many rooms. The ER, after I broke my hip. That terrible night of bright lights and needles and dozens of strange faces around my bed. Lying there, shivering, with my leg stuck out to the side like a broken tree branch. And pain? God!

Then, the hospital room. Later, the rehab place. Doctors, doctors, doctors to talk to. And long ago, there were other rooms—labor rooms, gynecologist's offices... I guess Max did his share—went into a few of those, at least.

It's almost eight feet away, but in that mirror next to the door, in that mirror I can see clearly my grey-brown face now. Doughy, crimped skin on the cheeks. But I'm so skinny now, neck like an old chicken, I think. Why is every mole, every lifted, red-brown lump on my face so clear? Can't see things close up anymore, and this is so clear. It scares me—my face.

I want to get up, go to the door, say something to the girl. Talk to her. Silly?

Doctor is moving on now--but not into here. I see the girl adjusting her shoulder bag. It's a meant-to-look-old, Coach, leather hobo pouch, I'm sure.

Suddenly, Nurse comes in. More X-rays I'm to have. No, no, I just had them. I'm not doing well: that's the problem. Complications. Too many surgeries, I think. Maybe another MRI this month, Nurse says.

Why did Doctor leave, anyway? Is it over? Oh, wait! He said he'd send Nurse in to get some information from me. Was it the nurse? They don't all dress like nurses.

"Just a minute," I say to her. I get up, pain still shooting through me like after the surgery. I lean on the walker, hands bruised from doing this, biceps and triceps strained from weeks of this. Months of this?

Outside the door, I see the girl. "Wait!"

She doesn't hear.

"Miss?"

She turns, balances on the good leg, positions the crutches carefully.

"Good luck to you," I say.

She comes closer. Now she looks so much like our Beth. Our Elizabeth, who we call Beth. Our Bethy. Boy, that fall day, in Ann Arbor. If they could've seen that. She was the college kid, and I almost beat her on the tennis court. I let her win, though. She knew I was better--even though she was twenty and strong. "Ma, you're the best," she said. "Don't have to do that."

Nurse is standing up now, I'm sure. Probably right behind me, at the door. I don't care, they think I'm bananas, anyway.

The girl gives me a toothy smile, and now, everyone, it seems, is looking at me.

"Good luck to you, too," the girl says and then starts to turn. But she swings back and I see that her eyes are bright, almost moist. We stare at each other. I think she understands that I don't want her to leave me here, with all these people. Don't leave me with Max. With Doctor, who makes me feel foolish and old. And ashamed.

Now my eyes are wet, too. But then, I'm going back in, and as I do, I can sense Doctor is somewhere in the corridor, looking at me.

Well, soon we'll be out of here--with orders and appointments for tests, with little cards to remind me of yet more visits. With prescriptions to fill. And Max will be mad, alright, and give me that nasty look because I still haven't told them they've misspelled my first name on their bill.

But screw it. Isn't that what our kids say? Screw the Doctor, too.

I think I could love that injured girl. I think I *was* that girl. I'll bet she knows. Well, maybe.

I am not so mad anymore, though. I'm thinking that tonight after Max goes to sleep, I'll stay up late, sit in the den, and eat that double chocolate cake. Cover it with ice cream. I'll watch Mary Tyler Moore and Bob Newhart and Taxi. Those people had values, those people I understand. Who cares about osteoporosis now? Can't ever get the bones back.

What does that girl think about me? About old people? Old, clawed, useless bags? People to respect? At the very least? Or was I just another old lady to be polite to? A lady who'd really be in her way if she hadn't found out for herself what it's like not to be able to walk.

Good luck to you, she said.

So now I am crying. Nurse is asking me questions, I realize. She stops asking, and puts a hand on mine. I try to stop crying.

Just then, Doctor pops his head in. "Appointment, a week to ten days after the tests," he reminds us.

Good luck to you...

Let's see now. If I sit on my bench in the shower tonight, I can wash myself, do my hair. Then put a clean gown over my useless hips and legs. It's okay, though. I'm starting to like this waiting-to-die, and all this thinking. In a way I hate it and in a way I love it. It's like I know something other people don't, have something inside it'll take them a lifetime to get. Too bad for them. Really.

Hey, Doctor. Listen, you *pisher* of a doctor. I was that girl. In case you didn't know, in case you forgot. And, you'll never know what I know. Okay?

Okay. So I'll fix myself up, and relax, and eat chocolate cake with ice cream. I'll watch good TV. I'll think. And I will stay up late into the night. Yes. Until then, I just have to get through the rest of this day.

TRIANGLE

ONE . . . . . Friday

With a hand on the binoculars, and the other pulling back the curtain at the foyer window, I look across the street and watch my sister Valerie slither up the front walk to her house. The new guy follows. New guy to her, but not to me. He trails dutifully, but with a cockiness, too, it seems, apparent even at that distance. Quick thing she is, leading him expertly. My younger sister Val--in her red flouncey dress, long but limp blond hair, chandelier earrings.

My knees lock and a small shudder starts inside as I wonder how many new positions she's shown him already.

Slowly, I let the curtain slide back and stare through the film of sheer material as their outlines disappear into the house.

"Ma?" Laura shouts from the direction of the kitchen doorway. "Ma, snap out of it. You're spying, like *Bubbe* does."

"Well, your Bubbe Sarah's not here, so I'll do it."

But I turn around, try to "snap out of it", frustrated, irritated, not exactly sure why I want to wait, and watch them maybe come out again. Maybe see them go to his car, which is parked at the curb.

"Laura, he was my doctor. I recognize him now. Jesus!"

"Think he knew that when they met?" she asks, walking toward me. "Or, early on?"

181

I pull my long brown hair into a twist and throw it over my shoulder. "How could he not have known? or guessed? It was only six or seven months, but I talked about Val."

"She told me they belong to the same ski club. Hiking stuff, too." Laura tugs at the African jewelry around her neck. "You know, I don't think Aunt Val's ever had a shrink for a boyfriend before."

"Honey, if he came here with her. I mean, he knows where we live."

"She probably slept with him before she mentioned who you were, and then..."

I think about a moment in his office two years ago when I gave in to an impulse to throw my arms around him. His body went rigid, but he didn't move away, either. But in spite of what I was trying, my desire suddenly disappeared and I didn't know what to do next. So I did nothing. It never happened again.

"Oh, wait," she says. "Wait, didn't we see him leaving the health club that time we went there with Val?"

"You're right. Oh, God, what a mess." I take a breath. "Of *course* they knew. One of them must've figured it out. Boy, it's such a different world now."

Suddenly, that office episode seems worse--resurrected.

"A different world now," I say again.

She frowns, looks at me for a few seconds, then rushes away toward the den in a flurry of long brown hair, oversized white shirt, and orthopedic sandals.

I follow her into the warmth of our den, into the array of earth tones that always comfort me here. I want her analysis of it now--what she thinks we should do about Val and the doctor.

Even when I thought I recognized him coming out of the house once before, in July, and even when Val mentioned that there was a serious new hunk, I didn't pry. It only *looked* like him that first time. I wasn't really interested. Then I went up to the Michigan Peninsula for two weeks. Laura took the train up to join me for the last week. And when we came back, there it was--Val bragging about it, about how great a relationship this was going to be.

I can't believe how much I like to confide in Laura these days, as if I were the kid. My baby, who's going to be a psychologist, is in her second year of grad school, and very committed to global causes. I tell her almost everything now.

We hash over the problem for a little while. Soon, I feel weepy, lost. Don't know why. But at least I'll be with Laura, my baby girl, for two more days before she goes away to school.

"Daddy just called," I say. "He's going to take the Outer Drive instead of Edens, so he'll probably be home in about an hour."

We sink into the off-white cushions of the sofa. I drop my sandals, dig my toes into the apricot carpeting. But now it flows into something else, something older than the Valerie stuff.

"I feel so damned uncomfortable with him lately, Laura." This is something I can tell her, too. "Sometimes, I wish he'd get tied up at the office like he used to all the time, or get stuck with a big case."

Uncomfortable with my husband? Not exactly. Richard and I are more like good roommates who have infrequent periods of acceptable, but unintimate sex. We are civil and friendly and very concerned with each other most of the time. Usual if you're in your forties? But we're still best friends, I'm sure of that. She doesn't start to analyze it today. She doesn't say anything. We curl up, her head on my shoulder, and look out the sliding glass door to the deck where the geraniums are blowing, bent over under a hot August wind.

Then, like someone's pushed the reset button, they shoot into my thoughts, intrude on my house and this mellow moment. Instant replay of the walk. I'm uneasy, anxious, feel like I'm being controlled by whatever is going on across the street.

Richard studies me with knitted brows. I decide to have another glass of the Chardonnay.

"Your sister is screwing *who?*" he asks as he pushes back against the slats of the oak dining chair.

"Steven Randall."

"No, Daddy," Laura says, "we're not completely sure."

"Oh, it's pretty obvious," I say.

"Sharon, whatever they're doing, if he's got a brain in his head..." Richard puts on what we know is his about-to-gather-the-facts-for-a-case attitude.

As I listen to him, I catch my pale, almost angry face in the mirror over the credenza. My eyes, too heavily lined in smudged violet-black tonight: my skin, rarely made up, covered with too much powdered bronzer. I'm an older version of Laura's strong glowing face.

"I have to do something about it, don't I, Rich? After all, we both saw him for counseling--me, longer than you."

"Call Aunt Val tomorrow, Mom," Laura says. "See what you can get out of her."

Richard stands up, announces he's going to change clothes, asks if we can have coffee and dessert out on the deck. I tell him it's fine, and start to stack the dinner plates, noticing that he's lost a little weight. But he's definitely the best looking, about-to-be-fifty-years-old guy at the health club. Great figure, still, without the weight-lifters bulge.

Still, I'm relieved that after coffee, and some talk that will be forced after Laura disappears into her room, I can tune everything out. I can get offstage.

"Maybe it's not as bad as we think," Laura says as we get things ready for the dishwasher. "Maybe it won't last."

I shake out the placemats in the sink, see the white plastic garbage can is full to bursting. I lift the bag out, twist tie the

bulge of garbage tightly. Have to get it
to the street before the truck comes in the
morning.

But impulse shoots me back to the
dining room table, and then to the hallway
leading to the master bedroom. "I didn't
say `screwing', Richard. *You* did. It's just
that I know something big's going on. And
it's worse than screwing. All of a sudden,
I can't stand it."

TWO . . . . . That Weekend

"Sharon, sweetie, I really can't talk
too long," Valerie says. "We're about to
have breakfast." Val is using that voice
she reserves for plumbers and salespeople,
or distant friends who call unexpectedly.
"How's everyone? Richard? Laura? Listen,
can I call you later?"

"Yes. Well, not at home, because I
have a lot to do today, and it's our last
weekend with Laura. Rich invited two couples
for the brunch tomorrow. Gotta get my hair
done."

"Oh, shoot," she says.

I know now she's being the darling
sister because he's listening. This morning
she has that I-just-love-everything tone.
The one she gets into when she's showing off-
-or hasn't come down from the three-orgasm
night. Or morning.

"We'll talk, Shar. I'll come see Laurie
before she gets on the plane. No, wait, I'll
try to come to brunch."

"Okay. Say, do I get to meet this person soon?"

"Sure...sure." She giggles. "Uh, we'll do it soon. I'm awfully busy at the shop, though. And I'm going out of town next week. His schedule is pretty tight now, too." A beep interrupts. "Oh, hold on, Shar, I got another call."

Val and our mom, Sarah, own a dress shop a few suburbs north of where we are. They carry more than dresses, and cater to a range of women from bank clerks to wealthy matrons, and their daughters. They offer image consultations, advice for travel wardrobes and trousseaus, and sometimes just general schmoozing. Mom devotes most of her time to it, gives it her all.

But Val isn't there as much as Mom. She'll study the books to see how the cash flow is going, make sure she's always around for trunk shows, go on big buying trips, but take off for exotic travel spots when the mood hits. Then Mom has to go there six days a week, slugging away with the same enthusiasm, the same work ethic she had as a young Polish girl who came to this country during the forties.

"Well, if you can tear yourself away, come for brunch tomorrow," I say to Val when she comes back on the line.

"Who's taking her to the airport?"

"Both of us. Tomorrow night."

"Maybe...maybe I'll make it, too. See, my friend, he'll be going home by then."

"Yeah? Okay, look, I gotta go, Val."

187

"Have a *great* day," she says.

I'm tempted to pick up the portable phone and the binoculars and run to the front hall even though I can't see her kitchen window from there. Maybe go outside and keep her talking? But Val's kitchen is on the side, with a greenhouse-style window in the breakfast area. I'd like to do it. Maybe they're naked.

Nuts to that. "Talk to you," is all I say and hang up.

I'm bending over the bathtub, giving it a decent scrub with a new Teflon sponge I found in the kitchen drawer. The Comet Cleanser I've sprinkled into the tub smells like bleach. My eyes smart as I inhale the green powder, that's now mixing with the thin layer of water in the tub. Scrubbing away in the corners, up around the rim, I sense Richard at the door. Maybe it's his aftershave, the pad of his bare feet. Something.

He comes up behind me. I'm only wearing a long tee--and it's riding up over my butt. I know what's next and brace myself. He pats me, kneels, pats me again, pushes his fingers up and around my thighs. Not possessively, not roughly, but just like he always does at the wrong moment. Or is it the wrong moment? Was it ever the wrong moment when we were young?

"Hey. Hey, Rich, I'm not showered. C'mon."

"Let's go in the bedroom, Sharon. Laura's out running with her girlfriends. She won't be back."

I turn slightly. The Comet-coated sponge drips and cleanser burns into the two paper cuts on my hand. "Hey, I'm not ready. I don't feel ready, don't feel beautiful yet."

"You're fine."

"Richard!"

He pouts.

He's home on Saturday for a change. No drive into Chicago to the office. A late morning and a slow, easy afternoon ahead. Things he never enjoys unless we plan a vacation. If he is off on a Saturday it's usually business mixed with golf, or business at the health club.

"Let me take a quick rinse off, Rich."

He smiles at me--white, even-toothed smile--grabs the oversize towel that we spread out on the bed for our less-than-spontaneous, bizarre sex routine. I won't come, I know. At least, not easily. Maybe it'll be bad. He'll feel I'm doing him a favor. We'll have to close the door because Laura might come back. Then he'll use his fingers, and I'll have to guide him, and we'll do it to me together, a little anxious because Laura just might come home in the middle of it. Not that she'd go ballistic if she caught us.

Why does this feel so blah? I wonder as he bobs up and down on top of me. His eyes are closed. Then he opens them and lowers onto one elbow. I bring my knees up higher. I still do love him, but it's not like it's supposed to be. So he lets a finger trail over my breast and it makes me quiver. I decide to help, run my own fingers over my backside, slide them under me. It works. I don't have to fake it. I have a sudden orgasm, without the buildup, without the heat. Like a quick burn, then a sadness that it's over and I'm back to sober so fast. Then he comes, too. Later, he holds me, says we should be together more.

On Sunday, as planned, we take the whole group to a restaurant for brunch, to a decadent spread--complete with champagne--at the Camelia Room in downtown Evanston. Val does come along. Without Dr. Randall, of course. She and Laura sit next to each other, talking girlishly, excessively. Mom has begged off, said she was tired, but will go to the airport with us later.

We have a huge table in the window corner, away from the rows of platters holding artistically arranged food that is fast being disarranged by the customers.

But Val and I don't bring it up. Richard looks like he wants to--even though there are two couples with us who are from his office. Not all family today, so we can't do it. It's over unless Val starts the ball rolling. But when we stand in line for the buffet all she says is that he's "wonderful" and everything will work out.

Of course *they've* talked about it by now, I'm sure.

So we eat, drink champagne, and "ooh" and "aah" at the different shapes they can put pates and smoked salmon into.

Val gets up for seconds now, or thirds--says she has to have more of the marinated baby asparagus and a slice of prime rib. I get up, too, going for more veggies, maybe some scrambled eggs. Rich smiles at me, and I offer to bring him a plate. He gives me a "Thanks, honey" and keeps talking to one of the couples--a new associate and his serious-faced chestnut-haired wife.

Amid diesel fuel smells and a very crowded waiting gate for Laura's plane, I feel weepy again. The empty nest? No. I'm used to that by now. Something else. More like the end-of-the-world, is-that-all-there-is feeling I had yesterday when he was so happy in bed and I felt sentenced to pleasant nothingness.

We hug and kiss Laura--all of us. I'm really bad by now. She smiles, says she'll write. Maybe, I think. But I know she'll call. Suddenly I picture her making love to someone. Hard to picture. Not hard to accept; just hard to picture.

That bastard Randall. I'm gonna have to call him tomorrow. Have to talk to him at his office.

THREE . . . . . Monday

Steven Randall is a tall but slightly-built man with smooth brown hair. His summer-tanned face wears a concerned look today as I sit across from him in his large inner city office. Huge hospital complex, really. A few buildings away is the psych ward, where he can shoot over to without even going outside.

So far he's been sympathetic to our "problem", but more like we're discussing someone else's, or a hypothetical.

The curved, black halogen lamp on his corner desk sprays bright light over a sea of carefully stacked papers. He sits in the other corner surrounded by a collection of watercolors on the wall, pictures I remember as if it were yesterday. Now, he's added rural scenes. They dot the wall above the patient's cozy, two-seat arrangement opposite him.

The arrangement Richard and I sat in, knees almost touching, and not wanting to touch, as we discussed, cried, pained out our dissatisfaction with each other. Rich was always more guarded, and waited before he spoke. I would just jump in, right after the pain in my chest would start at the thought of talking about my marriage.

But the anger, anxiety, that's been building in me on the drive down is sliding away. The overwhelming intimacy of this room, the intoxicating freedom I had back then to say whatever I wanted is sliding in.

I take a stab at it, anyway. "We have to talk, seriously."

"I'm not sure we should discuss this."

"But you said I could come here."

"You called this morning, made it sound like an emergency," he says, then sighs. "Mrs. Miller, it's been two years...and, uh, at first..."

He's stalling, I think. Trying to get through it by saying nothing. Really bullshitting me.

"Well, *now* you know, Doctor. I mean, I talked about her. Couldn't you--"

"Mrs. Miller, *she* wasn't my patient. And at first--"

"Sharon. You can call me Sharon again."

He leans back. "Sharon," he says calmly.

"Thrown together? Were you thrown together on the tennis courts? Or the health club? Couldn't help yourselves?"

"I don't think I have to justify that, here, this way." His voice is clipped now.

"Look, I don't want to hurt Val, but--"

"Neither do I," he says. "Let us--let Valerie and I talk about it."

"Just couldn't help yourself. Gotta go ahead when you're that turned on, right?"

"This isn't getting anywhere," he says.

Protecting himself. Just says enough and no more. No trigger points here. I'm fuming, but still mesmerized by our aloneness.

"So what if I wanted to do you in, Doctor?"

"Huh?"

"Hit you. Stab you. Patients *do* that, don't they?"

I lean forward to say more. He jumps--reflex jump with a simultaneous blink. Then he assumes the neutral pose again, but looks embarrassed, like someone who should've been better prepared for sudden moves, not given his response away.

"A joke," I say. "But, you know, my sister's so naive. She thinks if we talk about vibrators, or smoking joints, or how she's planning to go skiing with someone--you--that it makes her so sophisticated."

He lifts a brow, twists his hands outward, palms up.

I'm worried now that I've gone too far.

"This isn't appropriate at all," he says. "I understand how you feel."

"Do you? Listen, I said I don't want to hurt her."

"No?"

"No!"

"This really isn't getting anywhere, Sharon."

Now I don't like him calling me Sharon. "I said 'no.' Why would I want to hurt her? But you guys better talk."

FOUR . . . . . Tuesday

Val's house is dark, very dark. They're upstairs, for sure. At first I make noise to let them know I'm here, a little scared because I've let myself in to give her the new pillowcases I picked up for her at Marshall Field's.

How will I explain letting myself in? Say that I didn't see any cars in the driveway? Thought they were out and I heard Ginger barking? But Ginger is curled up around her rubber ball, dead to the world, her fat tummy heaving up and down in short, sleep-even breaths. She has an ear infection and has been sluggish for a week. Her ears perk up, though, and she is suddenly awake as I get closer to the stairs.

"Shh, hon," I whisper. "Shhhh."

She peers at me, then stretches out again, nose on the floor. Miraculous! Then she gives a little yip. "Shh," I say.

Noise now. From upstairs. "Oh, honey, oooh!" Val's voice groans from the direction of the master bedroom.

I freeze.

"Oh, *God!*" she screams.

Now he's groaning, and just about screaming, too. "Val, Val." And then a sound like, "Urghhh." So loud.

I picture them squeezing against each other, then pulling back, and slapping together again--her thin, big boned anatomy swelling, sassy. They're sticky, and together. And free. No wedding rings flashing in the dim light.

My breath is short now. I let it come, don't hide it like when Rich and I are watching porn. I want to go up and see those glowy, confused aftermoments.

Things are moving around up there now. Shishing noises. Squeaks. The bedroom door squeals it's special sound because the post doesn't fit into the hinge just right. One of them is coming out. Ginger stirs, barks, her nose twitching. A dream, they'll think she's having a bad dream. She looks toward me, pants a little. But no one's in the hall, no one at the top of the stairs yet.

What am I doing?

"Bye, baby," I whisper to Ginger. Nervously but carefully, I head toward the kitchen door, then out.

As I push through the head-high bushes that separate Val's lot from the Smiths, next door, I break out in a sweat. No cars in the driveway here, though. I'm safe. No lights, either. But the lights do go on in Val's kitchen, and, mercifully, go out again.

Thank God the bedroom faces front, I think, crossing the Smiths' backyard, keeping close to the bushes. They'd have to move fast, into the rec room, to see me at all now. Bet they didn't do it. So I stand, cower, feet in the rain-soaked trough of grass at the edge of the lot, where the backyard meets another that belongs to a house on the next street west of our's.

Soon, I think about how lucky I was to get away. Lucky no one saw me. Slipping through backyards, even if the lights are out and the cars are gone—you could get shot doing that.

So I trudge around, my rubber thongs squishing, sucking against the wet sidewalks, and finally, I escape north, onto Church Street. No more side streets. Lots of traffic on Church now. Then I pick up the pace--like I *always* exercise this way, always take fast walks in bad weather, in the dark rain.

It seems an eternity as I try to get farther away, zigzagging up and down streets more familiar by car than on foot. No ID on me, bare legs, no bra under the tanktop. I'm cold now. It's settling in slowly. What have I done? I'm shaking cold now. I have to go back home.

I go past colonials on double lots, swimming pools hidden in back. Past not-so-modest, four bedroom palaces with cathedral-ceilinged foyers. Past places with huge room additions for the kids in the family--to give them everything the parents never had. Like the boomer parents ever had it that bad anyway.

Richard is going to be home any minute, if he isn't already, I'm thinking as I finally get near our street. But I want to run in the house now, be alone, put my legs up, look at myself, touch myself...

So why does she make me feel so weird? So wild?...so nothing?

Now I'm standing on our front walk. For a good five minutes, I stand there. Then I see our car turning down the street, coming south, from Church.

Across the street in Val's living room, there's light. The curtains move. I pray it's only Ginger.

Richard stares up at me. He has five-o-clock shadow and didn't take a shower because I wouldn't wait for that. Couldn't wait, or I might've changed my mind.

He can't get hard, though. I don't care. It feels better than I thought it would. I'll get all the right places, wriggling, pressing. So I pin his arms back, gently. He seems surprised, seems to like this.

From somewhere across the street, or out in the street, Ginger is barking. Must be her. First: close, loud yelps, then: farther away sounds, like she's gone in back, to play in her doghouse.

I turn up the volume on the clock radio. A group is singing. Peppy stuff. But I don't care if it's fast or slow, or what we listen to now. Smiling at Richard, all the while careful to keep my chin up, face muscles tightened, I sink slowly onto his flesh. Carefully. Until he gets hot, really carried away, he's going to notice every detail on my sagging face.

FIVE . . . . . Wednesday
"Isn't he smart enough to cover it up?"

A young voice. But with a sound of new confidence that some women get when they share the excitement, the experiences of working in a big law firm. Of working side by side with the harried lawyer. Knowing a side of him that his wife doesn't.

"He doesn't have to worry," someone shouts back from the direction of the sink or counter.

Neither gal sounds like Sally, Richard's thirty-something secretary. So I unroll four sheets of toilet paper, wrap it around my hand, cough a little, not knowing whether to stay and find out who "he" is, or come out.

Water runs. Then the snap of paper towels being pulled from the dispenser. It's all whispering now. Then a squish like hairspray, and the door opens, and their voices go farther away.

I come out, wash, run a comb through my hair, tease the top a little. Suddenly I feel foolish, wonder who I have to stop and say hello to. How many partners should I pop in on? And just for protocol, how many associates? Richard's old wife says, Hello. Do they ever laugh? Call me the old broad? How bad would he have to look to get called the old *cocker*?

I don't stop and visit, just smile at people.

God, has he told anyone we're having problems? Hinted? News travels fast and people don't respect your privacy anymore. Especially the secretaries, who are either old crackerjacks with lined but carefully made-up faces, or young, creamy-skinned, well-toned babes who all want to be paralegals or go to law school at night. One bright-eyed young girl actually asked me at the last Christmas party who Dick van Dyke was. She made me feel that Rich had another world to live in, one where "old stuff" meant it was from the eighties.

I go down the hall to Rich's office, which has a soft beige couch, medium-priced Oriental rug on the floor, and my and Laura's picture on the desk.

I open the door. The bright northeast light high above La Salle Street, and the Chicago River a block away, fill my view.

"Hi, hon," Richard says cheerfully, standing up. "I called Sorriso's. Over on the river? Okay?"

"Sure. I'm early. I'll just collapse here 'til you're through."

He makes a big production of clearing space on the couch--even though there was only one folder on it and someone's umbrella resting against the side.

"Gotta go to Dave's office," he says. "Back in a minute."

Just after he leaves I hear Sally laugh, and him saying something to her I can't quite pick up. Today her laugh is like Val's-- slightly provocative, sassy.

Not my Richard, I think. Not my Richard.

Suddenly I picture Val's face. And I'm hot, out of my skin now. Then I picture Dr. Steven Randall's face. All of a sudden, I really don't feel so good.

"You're the one who told Val about the house across the street," Rich says.

I look down at the river below us. "I know."

I watch the traffic down there. Sailboats and motorboats are gliding through the greenish waters of the Chicago River, their shapes disappearing temporarily as they go under the drawbridges.

After a sip of wine and a long pause, I can't come up with more, except for, "Do you know what she said to me at the party?"

Richard sighs. "No, what?"

"She said, 'I don't know what you guys see in this place. Why'd you make it here?'"

"So?"

"So, that's terrible."

"Look, Val is Val," he says. "Don't you know her by now?"

"I didn't make the party for her. It was Laurie's. I--"

"Then why didn't you tell her--"

"I did." I curl my fist against my thigh. "I tried to."

He looks very business-like now, leans back in his chair. "Shar, you let her push your buttons. It's a game with her sometimes." He lowers his voice as our waitress comes toward the table. "She doesn't even know she's doing it."

"She knows."

Silence. We are both silent until the food arrives.

I'm waiting now for examples of his ideas of real stress. Waiting for how this should be nothing much for me. How *he* gets up at five every day, after not sleeping half the night sometimes because he's anxious over a court date. Anxious over how he'll handle a new client's case. Then he'll add that I should forget it. If you can't change it, forget it. Consider the source, and all that crap.

But you're not a sister, Rich. You don't know.

We eat our lunch, mostly in silence. No advice from him this time. We go through the ritual of sharing--I give him some of my salad and he shovels spoonfuls of pasta onto my plate.

A cloudless blue sky today. Temps in the seventies. People, flowers, leafy plants everywhere. The downtown buildings canyoning around us. It should've been an upper.

When we're almost through, a few words I can't swallow down with the food pop out. "Easy for you to say." Instantly I'm sorry. But still no lectures from him. We just finish our lunch under that bright blue, cloudless sky.

Later, up on street level, he kisses me goodbye, and says, "Straw that broke the camel's back?"

"What?"

"Randall. The Randall thing."

I can only smile at him, suddenly pleased, comforted that he knows me so well. I reach up and hug him. Long hug. "See you tonight."

After he walks away, I keep standing there. When he is part way across the bridge, he looks back, waves, and then heads south to the office.

The phone rings as I'm walking along Wacker Drive.

"Hello?"

"Hi, it's Val."

"I was going to call you." Almost forgot she's going away and I'm supposed to look after Ginger.

"I thought I'd do it before I started packing. Well, if you can take care of Ginger, and feed her something, you know, that you can slip her pills into. I would appreciate it."

"Don't worry, I'll take her to our house."

"See, my friend and I--well, we're going up to Door County," she says.

"Neat." But I'm bristling as I say it.

"He's only got a few days," she tells me. "It's close enough, and so beautiful."

Beautiful, yes. If your left hand were the state of Wisconsin, your thumb would be where the Door Peninsula is. We went there as teenagers, young marrieds. And long ago, some of the resorts were so homey, the waitress would come out of the kitchen and say, "Tonight we're having whitefish." And you didn't want anything else, it was so good.

Now, there are more marinas. More people. Condos. A road that used to end at water's edge without much fanfare now has distracting man-made additions. Still, it's beautiful--Lake Michigan on one side and Green Bay on the other...

"Shar? Are you there?"

"Yes, I'm here."

"Okay, so--"

"Valerie, listen.   It's him, right? Dr. Randall?"

Quiet on her side. But Ginger starts to bark. "Yes, okay, yes. But you knew that already. Right?"

"Couldn't you have told me?"

"Sharon, don't you want me to be happy? I mean--"

"Happy, yes. But this is different." Did she find out I went to his office this week?   "Val, you must have realized that I used to see him, talked about stuff. About you, too."

"It just happened," she shouts.

"All you had to do was tell me."

"But you're so touchy."

"Touchy?"   I look around, worried now that people are looking at me, but most of them seem to be shouting into their phones, too.

"Everything tics you off, you're so moody, difficult," she goes on.

I'm getting short of breath. There's a pressure starting under my skin. I sink down onto the nearest concrete bench, along the riverwall, and stare at a planter that's full to bursting with flowers.

"I'm not going to deprive myself of this," she says. "What do you want from me, Sharon? What?"

My head is swimming, but it comes out, with an awful struggle. "I want--I want *respect*. Do you understand? Do you?"

Ginger starts barking again.

"Well," she says, as if groping for the right words, "well, didn't I tell all my friends about how hard it was for you? How you had Laurie when Rich was still in law school?"

"That's not--"

"Oh, why didn't you just have more, so you wouldn't be butting your nose in someone else's business. And always judging me."

"More? Have more? They fixed that, remember?"

"Oh, yeah," she says more quietly. "I forgot for a..."

My heart is pounding in my ears. "Forgot? You forgot? You acted like they only took my appendix out!"

So short of breath now. I look up, out to the wide sidewalk in front of me. This time people are staring.

"I want respect from you from now on," I say.

I barely hear the click as Valerie hangs up on me.

When I get off the train I'm so tired I can't make the legs move. Always try to do the six block walk home on foot to enjoy the shady streets, the smell of fresh cut grass. Like to come down after a day in the downtown crowds. But I do make it to the back door, then into the kitchen. My legs still feel wobbly, as if I just had the wine from lunch.

Before I get close to the table, I see a note taped to it. Even at a distance I recognize Val's big printing:

"Shari,

Thank you so much for agreeing to take care of Ginger.

I do appreciate it. She has a vet Appt. on Fri. but if it's too much trouble, just let it go. I'll try to bring back some cherry preserves. I know how you like anything with Door Cty. cherries in it.

Val--"

I take the note, turn and head for the den. My shoes come off just after I sink into the sofa. The sofa where Laurie and I had cuddled less than a week ago. Seems more like a year ago.

It's not going to be easy with Val. Going to be hard.

Almost six o'clock. Rich will be home any minute now. On the desk, across from where I'm sitting, sits a menu from the pizza place we like. It'll be Greek pizza tonight. One of our favorites. Black olives and lots of feta.

I'm still holding the note.

Thank you for the favor, and Door County cherries--Val's version of an apology. I read it again, pour over it, looking for between-the-lines words of love.

Then it dawns on me. My life with Rich, with Laura, with anyone, is like the bottom of a triangle, with Val on the top. She intrudes on my thoughts, she gets to me. It's worse than Rich thinks. Worse than I ever realized. Going on for so long, too, and getting to be more each day.

I know I have to break it, break this pattern. The phone call was a start. Now, she knows. And I know that "consider the source" won't do anymore. So, the ball is still in her court.

I crumple the note in the palm of my hand. Then, I get up and drop it into the wastebasket.

Not going to be easy at all, I'm thinking as I pick up the pizza menu. But nothing important ever is.

Printed in the United States
24505LVS00001B/136